Prai

"Every parent encounters some chasm between the ideal child they imagined and the actual child they are raising. With aching honesty and profound generosity, Rachel Stolzman Gullo delivers a beautifully written novel about one family traversing that divide and learning to love one other, not as they might be but as they are. The result is a deeply humane novel that lingers long after the last page is turned."
GAYLE FORMAN, NEW YORK TIMES BESTSELLING AUTHOR OF *IF I STAY*

"A heart-wrenching, deftly told, story, that reminds us that sometimes you have to break a thing before you fully understand how it works. Rachel Stolzman Gullo hands us the broken pieces of a family, and the glue to put it back it back together again, shard by jagged shard. Bring your hankies. You're going to need them."
COLIN BRODERICK, AUTHOR OF *CHURCH END*

"Poignant, brave, and utterly gorgeous. Stolzman Gullo has crafted a wonderful, strange, and astounding masterpiece. Just when I thought I knew where this compelling novel would go, I was proven wrong. Read this book. Then read it again. You won't be able to put it down."
AMANDA BOYDEN, AUTHOR OF *I GOT THE DOG*

"I read in great gulps. Stolzman Gullo has written a love song to love itself, as sturdy and astounding a thing, it turns out, as a well-designed skyscraper, built to confuse the wind."
AMY HASSINGER, AUTHOR OF *AFTER THE DAM*

About the Author

Rachel Stolzman Gullo is the author of two prior novels, *The Sign for Drowning* and *Practice Dying*. She earned an MFA in Creative Writing from Sarah Lawrence College. She works in New York City in the field of public health. She lives with her husband and their two children in Brooklyn.

rachelstolzman.wordpress.com

Confuse
the Wind

Rachel Stolzman Gullo

www.vineleavespress.com

For Penny and Tsvi

1.

Jonathan stood in the dark by the window. The sun would be up soon. He waited there to save Theo the trip down the long hallway. Every day Theo woke at eleven minutes to sunrise. These days he was waking at 5:56. But he would shift the time as the days wore on, to pace the sun. This was one of the mysterious depths that Jonathan marveled at about his son. What did his circadian rhythms mean? These invisible pulleys that tied him to the earth.

Jonathan didn't enjoy waiting there in the half-light or being awake. He puzzled with the engineering option he'd selected for the topmost five stories of his current skyscraper project, work that would commence later that day. He was certain the best architectural choice for this building consisted of venting with minimal surface variation. Skyscrapers used a combination of engineering techniques to defy physics, to stand tall for centuries. All great skyscrapers had a personality and said something to all who looked at them. This residential project, a twenty-six-story skyscraper in Gramercy Park, The Jetson, would have a personality too. Jonathan pushed with every design choice to give a building its true form. His buildings tended to garner local notoriety and appreciation but weren't famous skyscrapers discussed around the world. Jonathan wanted The Jetson to be appreciated for exactly what it was: for its marriage of form and function.

Jonathan had taken a state job sixteen years ago because he believed in oversight and not in profit when it came to development. Later he stayed on for the health insurance, sick days, and paid vacations. For the health insurance that covered all of Theo's therapies and a pension to help support Theo forever and ever. The job often made him feel like an administrator, not an engineer. But it was his nature and passion to find the simplest design. Every skyscraper had a core essence, a truth that could be unveiled and brought to its surface, and he never tired of finding it.

Somehow, he hadn't seen him coming. Theo landed against his shin. He'd had a growth spurt and he rocked Jonathan with his physical arrival. There was time, years earlier, when Theo ran down this hallway, his arms held aloft for balance, to land against his father's body. Jonathan felt the burst of affection that seeing Theo always brought him.

"Hi, Boomer. You found me. I guess the sun's coming up. Sun—eleven minutes!" Jonathan called out like a department store elevator man from bygone days.

Theo smiled up at him, his baby and few adult teeth a shamble of gaps and stones. His dark-blond wavy hair needed cutting again. Theo's wideset eyes were his mother's shape and Jonathan's shade of green. His face had perfect symmetry and for that was considered beautiful. Theo's outstretched hand held a pair of clean underwear.

"Good thinking, Theo. You hate sleeping in a diaper, and I hate it too." Jonathan couldn't help it. He squatted beside his boy, resisting lifting him up. He kissed Theo's head in the tangle of his hair that smelled clean from the shampoo he'd used to wash his hair the night before. "Let's go get you dressed." Jonathan walked back to his room and Theo followed on the floor with his preferred style of locomotion, the scoot, one knee raised up, the other leg pushing against the floor like a swimmer.

"You're my big boy." The words sounded benign, but they caused tension in his gut because he was thinking, he's seven already, and here we still are.

"Pink Posey."

"Whoa. You're talking early today."

Theo curled like a mermaid, twisting to look at his toenails that Aimee had painted for him. Jonathan noted some bruises on his bent knees.

"Is that the color?" Jonathan asked. He was aware that girls and boys were equally permitted painted toenails in Brooklyn in 2023, but he wondered briefly why Aimee took every liberty. Was it perhaps an old nail polish that Carly had left behind when she'd moved out?

In Theo's room, Jonathan flipped on the light and plopped Theo back on his bed. In this moment it would be used as a changing table. He playfully counted his son's toes, sending the little piggie off to the market, and then quickly removed his nighttime diaper, fortunately just wet.

—

Theo's first few months of life are a blur to Jonathan. His memories are impressionistic, a series of images and feelings embedded in all his senses. He remembers noticing Theo's biceps right after he was born. How does a newborn have biceps? Carly ran a finger over one of his tiny arms in the hospital bed as he curled into her side, searching for her nipple.

"He must have been climbing the walls in there." Carly laughed happily.

They were mesmerized by his uniqueness. His lips seemed muscular, and he nursed on the first try, like he'd done it for years. Then they noticed his wrinkled thumb and realized he'd been sucking in the womb. His eight-pound body was relaxed and sanguine from day one. When Jonathan buried his nose in his son's neck, Theo's scent was earthy and nutty, his breath smelled milky. The weight and smell and warmth of Theo's tiny body became Jonathan's security blanket, lain across his chest. Once home, Theo lay sprawled in a bouncy seat and looked around the room. He held their gaze for minutes on end.

Theo picked up small objects with his pointer finger and thumb when he was barely three months old. Jonathan read about the "pincer grasp." It was a fine motor skill that should come later. He wished it was acceptable to tell the whole world about Theo's pincer grasp.

Theo delighted them endlessly. He sat up like a tripod at five months of age, balancing on his bottom and diamond-shaped legs, his arms catching him whenever he wobbled. His favorite thing to do was play with wooden letter blocks. He lined them up, he stacked them, he sucked on them, he threw them. Jonathan and Carly read about everything he did. He was training in physics. Cause and effect were also in his curriculum. He was developing binocular vision by crawling to his blocks. Jonathan became an amateur anthropologist, constantly looking to see why his beautiful boy did the things he did. Every action and behavior had a purpose. And yet still, it all seemed to be just Theo. Or Theo was a miracle anyway. Because he was him, and only him.

When Theo got his first teeth at six months, the lower middle two, Jonathan and Carly learned that every human gets those two teeth first. Totally miraculous and totally ordinary. Jonathan wondered how this could be, day after day.

They introduced rice cereal, sweet potato, apples, carrots, scrambled eggs, and peanut butter to stave off allergies. One at a time, like the books implored. How else would you know what they were allergic to? Jonathan didn't discover until much later that babies all around the world ate stews with more than fifteen ingredients and were fine.

They had planned on not letting Theo "cry it out." If he couldn't sleep they would go to him, over and over. Soothe him and then leave him, again and again. They would outlast him. But he was a freakishly good sleeper. Once he stopped nursing at midnight and 4 a.m., he slept through the night. Again, Jonathan wondered if he could walk the streets telling strangers what his boy could do. He'd brag only to Carly though, and she would agree. Theo is the best of all time. She meant it, but she also held that all children were the best of all time. She loved kids and babies universally, always had. Jonathan found his first love for a baby in his own.

Theo stood in his crib at nine months, holding the bars and roaring for his parents at 6:00 a.m. The front side of the crib was soon covered in teeth marks from Theo sinking his new baby teeth into the wood.

He always smiled when one of them came to his rescue. A big, open, drooly smile. His wet diaper sagged, knees bouncing with joy that the sun had come up yet again. Lifting Theo out of the crib and blowing a berry against his skin filled Jonathan with a feeling not far from euphoria. His body echoed Theo's joy. Miraculous and ordinary.

Theo began walking at one. Which surprised Jonathan for its averageness. With all of Theo's muscles and gross and fine motor skills, Jonathan had been waiting for months already. But at one, Theo took off, and then at one and a day, he started running. Jonathan and Carly learned how to chase their child down the sidewalk. Another new thing, always another new thing.

Theo's first birthday party was held in Prospect Park. They had more friends without kids than with. Twenty-odd adults came, five kids of various ages. There was a silver number one balloon and a rainbow of smaller balloons. Bagels and cupcakes and beer. Theo rode about the party in the crook of Jonathan's right arm for hours. When they sang, Theo nestled in Carly's arms, sang along too, "Ha tu tu, to Tee-ooo, ha tu tu to you." He blew on a single candle but couldn't blow it out.

Jonathan and Carly kissed on the mouth as though it was their wedding day again, causing their friends to hoot and laugh at them. Jonathan felt lucky being him.

—

While Theo still lay on his bed, Jonathan opened his dresser drawer and pulled out blue pants and a dark green cotton t-shirt. He dressed Theo efficiently, pulling the t-shirt over his head and steering his hands while the boy pushed his arms through the armholes. Jonathan pulled the fabric down and gave his boy's tummy a pat.

"You hungry for breakfast?"

"Ha tu tu." Theo sang.

"Ha tu tu? Whose birthday is it now?"

"Ha tu tu, to Dada." He had the melody just right, another cognitive mystery to Jonathan.

"Thank you, sweetie, but my birthday's months away. Up and at 'em. Aimee will be here soon."

Jonathan strapped Theo into his chair. He poured milk over Cheerios and peeled a banana, slicing it into his bowl. He handed him a toddler spoon with a fat handle, easier for gripping.

"Hold on, sorry, Theo." He apologized while snapping the bib around his seven-year-old's neck.

Jonathan rushed through setting up his French press while, miraculously, Theo fed himself. He rushed so he could sit with him and push himself to talk, to stimulate Theo's mind, to relax a little and not race to the moment he could remove Theo's bib and clean him up.

—

When Theo was fourteen months old, Carly frantically called Jonathan at work one afternoon. "Theo's got a fever."

"Oh, yeah? A new tooth?"

"I don't think so. He's upset. Really agitated."

"What? Like what?" *Had they ever seen Theo really agitated?*

"He's so hot and he's kind of thrashing in his crib."

Jonathan put his pen down. He could picture Theo doing a thousand different things he'd seen him do for four hundred some days. Thrashing wasn't one of them. Jonathan realized he could hear Theo over the phone, mewling like a tomcat.

"Pick him up, Carly."

"I've been holding him all day! He's been thrashing in my arms and I just put him down to call you. Hold on."

Carly's cellphone made a thud on the table and then silence. Jonathan strained to make out the mewling. There was silence. He stood and started packing his bag to leave. His gut churned, and his hands filled with sweat.

She came back.

"Jonathan? He's asleep. But he doesn't look like he fell asleep. He looks like he passed out."

"Call the doctor, Carly. We can meet at the pediatrician's office. Has he had Tylenol?"

"I was about to give him some, but I didn't yet. He's very hot. His face is all pink. Maybe he's just sleeping." Carly's voice was far away.

"I'm leaving work. Call the pediatrician. I can meet you guys there."

When Jonathan came above ground in Brooklyn, he saw he'd missed two calls from Carly. He called her immediately.

"Jonathan, we're in a car service on our way to Methodist. He's awake again but totally listless. The doctor said to go to the ER."

"The ER?"

"Yes, they don't handle emergencies."

"Is this an emergency?"

"I don't know! It's not normal Theo."

"I'll get an Uber and meet you at Methodist."

—

The next seventy-two hours are days that Jonathan can't bear to look back on. Theo's fever rose to 106 °. He was dark pink and for a full day medicine wouldn't bring his fever down. He was listless and once or twice thrashing and agitated. He couldn't eat, or nurse, or drink water, and was given an IV even before he left the ER.

Once admitted to the ICU, he was transformed into a pediatric patient. His clothes disappeared. His body was insanely small in his pediatric gown in a hospital bed. He had a stent in his left forearm and an IV on a pole. Those sweet biceps could do nothing to help him fight an invisible enemy. Nutrition was forced through a feeding tube twice. Luckily he nursed breast-milk after forty-eight hours. Carly cried, a new set of tears, different from the tears that had been coming for two days already. Cried that he wasn't the same nurser. His suck was all different.

The hardest thing was that his eyes and facial features changed. It seemed his eyes hollowed so they seemed less indented, his face became more of a smooth surface. In the dark, Jonathan thought his face looked like a potato. He banished the thought in shame.

And it turned out the change in facial features was the telltale sign. He had a virus that Jonathan and Carly had both heard of but never learned a thing about. Theo had encephalitis. The virus was causing swelling of his brain. Had he been an infant still, his soft spot would be protruding to allow space. As it was his eyes seemed pressed from the inside. His body was limp and exhausted from fighting off this new life form that didn't belong.

The fever waned one degree at a time. 105°, 104°, 103°. They rejoiced with each decreasing number. It was like when they had celebrated Carly's dilation—three centimeters, four centimeters, five; The baby is coming!

Jonathan took to laying in the hospital bed; Theo curled into his side. Jonathan held and stroked him, whispering into his hot ear.

"You're okay, my boy. It's going away now."

He and Carly took turns lying in bed with Theo. Carly would unbutton her shirt and Theo would suckle on-and-off for hours, like a newborn. Every drop of breast milk seemed like precious medicine. Jonathan caressed Carly's leg and watched. He was so grateful she hadn't stopped nursing yet. There was all-powerful breastmilk to bring Theo back.

Encephalitis hits like a flu. There's fever, muscle aches, loss of appetite, fatigue.

"It will pass in a few weeks," the doctors said.

They didn't need to hear more. They were going to get out of this.

Theo was discharged at last. They went home. The fever and other main symptoms loosened their grip on Theo, released him. He was back to eating and drinking in his high chair. He was back to surveying the room and holding their gaze for long minutes. He was even back to babbling words and smiling happily. But he wasn't standing in his crib, or walking, or running. They kept this secret for a few days. It had been four hellish days in an ICU. They had already been told the virus would take a few weeks to recede. He was Theo again, just a somewhat younger Theo.

Eight days after the fever had hit him, they decided they should tell the pediatrician he wasn't standing or walking anymore. It was also hard for Theo to sit up and play with his blocks. The sturdy tripod pose he'd mastered at six months was hard to obtain now. He seemed weak.

Carly was still upset with the call she'd made to the only pediatrician they'd ever known. "It was bizarre, Jonathan. As soon as I said he was really sick, high fever, they basically said go to the ER and hung up. Aren't they doctors? I always thought that they work with sick kids. What's up—do they only do well visits and shots?"

"It is weird. But we're not going to call the ER with our concerns. Who else would we call?"

Jonathan called Theo's doctor himself. The doctor called him back promptly and Jonathan found himself, for the first time, retelling the entire story from the first signs of distress. The doctor didn't really know anything about Theo or his episode. Theo Brooks had not been a memorable patient; he was just a computer file of a fourteen-month-old—a growth chart and vaccine history.

Jonathan felt silly talking so long, as though he thought the pediatrician was a close friend. But he also couldn't stop. Speaking about what they'd been through and the progression of the illness, the changes that had overcome Theo, was suddenly an emotional need and outlet. He had to tell the story and there was no short version.

"Encephalitis." The doctor said with some interest. For him, the story boiled down to one word. A diagnosis. Here's what medical school training could do. Jonathan could feel the doctor Googling over the phone.

"Yeah. Well that's what we've been told. Anyway, he's better now. He's recovered. But he's a bit worn down. He's regressed perhaps." Jonathan looked at Carly. He hadn't prepared for what this call was. Carly widened her eyes at him and raised her hands. She wanted him to do better, but he wasn't sure what he was asking anymore.

"Theo's not standing up or walking yet. He was walking and even running. He's fourteen months. As you know."

"How many days has it been since the fever commenced?"

Commenced. Jerk.

"Eight days."

"I'm not too worried." Theo's one-and-only doctor said calmly. "That's a powerful virus. And a virus affects everyone differently. It takes weeks for a virus to work its way out, up to six weeks. You may see new phases, rash, diarrhea. But I want to hear any changes. Give him another week to regain his stamina and muscle strength. Call me if he's still not up and about in a week or four days."

Well which is it? Jonathan was not imprecise. "So four days or a week?"

The doctor was improvising and Jonathan was infuriated by it. He wished he wasn't picturing the guy in medical school, learning about encephalitis for five minutes.

"You can call me in four days. But he needs time to regain his strength."

"Thanks Doctor." Jonathan hung up. "Motherfucker," he said to Carly. "But it sounds normal. The virus can take weeks to work itself out. He was hit hard." Jonathan walked away from his cell phone and approached Carly on the couch, where she sat with Theo tucked against her. Jonathan reached out his hands and picked Theo up. Theo wrapped his arms around his dad's neck. His lower body settled into Jonathan's torso. Jonathan gently squeezed his beautiful boy.

Six months after the illness, Theo was almost two years old. They'd long since left their pediatrician in Carroll Gardens, who they'd painfully discovered didn't work with children with prolonged illnesses. They were at their third visit to a specialist at Mount Sinai, a prestigious teaching hospital in Manhattan.

The specialist, Dr. Wyatt, had been well-vetted before their first appointment. They would not fall blindly into a doctor's care ever again. Dr. Wyatt had multiple specializations in pediatrics and neurology. And most importantly, they trusted her. Carly had sat Jonathan down after her hours of research on doctors in New York.

"Jonathan, she's the best. She's twenty years out of medical school, thank God, I can't take another doctor who is still in puberty. She's a pediatric neurologist. She even knows encephalitis. But here's the deal: *we* are never going to know the medical answers. This isn't your field; it's not what we know." She went on very slowly. "We have to trust the doctor we choose. That's the way to survive this."

"Yes, of course. I'm aware I'm not a doctor." Jonathan shut his mouth but his mind still raced. He couldn't resist the caveat that he knew made all the difference. "But we are the Theo experts."

"Jonathan, don't always have the last word."

After their first visit with Dr. Wyatt they both agreed that they did trust her. And they relied on her assessment of Theo. They often hung on her every word, repeating to each other for days afterwards how she had described the healing process. How Theo might recover.

At two, Theo underwent a work up of every system. Blood work, EKG, CT scan, X-rays, reflexes, vision, hearing. And a cognitive evaluation that took two days to administer.

Sitting in Dr. Wyatt's office, Carly and Jonathan held hands. They had less than three minutes in the room before she entered.

"Are you nervous?" Carly asked.

"I'm prepared to hear the worst. There's no reason to be holding out hope for good news. She isn't going to tell us he's fine. We see that Theo fell off track. He's not progressing; he's regressing. There's no news to be told here."

Carly gasped. She didn't have time to say or even form a rebuttal before Dr. Wyatt entered the room and sat behind her desk.

Before she spoke, Dr. Wyatt looked at the couple before her. Jonathan saw himself and his wife through her eyes. She could readily see Carly's bloodshot eyes and Jonathan's armor and pout. He tried to sit up taller. His slouch was insolent.

"Hi, Carly. Hi, Jonathan. Theo did great. He was really cooperative and tireless."

She cares about Theo. Jonathan nearly chanted this new mantra in his thoughts over her words.

"In rare cases of encephalitis, it takes months to resolve the injuries to the brain. He's a very healthy child. Robust. Every virus has its own load, its own lifespan. He needs more time. And I'm referring you for physical therapy and speech therapy. It will be three sessions a week for each. You can bring him to the therapists or they can come to your home. It's a full load."

"And he still might catch up?" Jonathan asked despite himself, his voice catching in his throat.

"To other kids? That's a bit of mythology. The range of normal development is huge. There's no exact standard to catch up to. Some kids talk when they're three, some at one."

"No." Carly paused for so long that Jonathan thought she had nothing else to say but "no." "Will he catch up to Theo? Will he catch up to himself before he was hit by a ton of bricks?"

Dr. Wyatt nodded. "I don't know. There's a lot of work ahead of him."

—

Jonathan came to the table with his own bowl of yogurt and granola, his cherished Peruvian coffee, and finally sat down.

"You want more, Theo?"

"Nana."

"You want banana?"

Theo shook his head. He was just noting that there were bananas in the bowl in front of him.

Theo began to speak at three. Not conversation, but "words in English," as Jonathan put it to Carly and his sister Emily, the only two people he opened up to about Theo. And once his words were coming, Jonathan found that with effort and repetition, his vocabulary could grow. Since Jonathan could achieve progress in this area, he worked hard at it. When he returned home at 6 p.m. each evening, Theo was pretty much deposited in his arms. He would lay on the rug with him while Carly got a glass of wine, opened her computer, stared, and sipped. Jonathan would talk and talk.

"How was your day, Boomer? Did you play today? Who did you see? I missed you."

He felt as though Theo was gifting him if he said, "Day," or "Book," or "Play," or "Dada."

In the tub, the repetition continued. "Ducky wants to play with Theo. Is this your duck? Look at Mr. Yellow Duck. Quack. Quack. Who says quack? Duck!"

And after hours of this, over weeks, Theo might say, "Duck."

Jonathan estimated that Theo had a vocabulary of three hundred words, and he was a pro at echoing back almost any word-sound. At seven he spoke just like a two-year-old, which was an accomplishment.

—

"Book on the chowch."

Theo used a handful of pronunciations that Jonathan found too sweet to correct and instead he adopted his boy's version.

"Oh, yeah, you're done? Okay, let's read a book on the chowch."

Jonathan unhooked the straps on Theo's Stokke chair. He was grateful when he found furniture or gear that worked for Theo that also met his aesthetic preferences. He placed his son on the floor.

"Get a book, I'll bring my coffee and read to you."

He watched Theo scoot to the bookcase and trace one finger along the lower shelf of his picture books, imitating him.

But before he could finish his black coffee, the doorbell rang. It was 6:30 a.m. and Theo's nanny, Aimee, had arrived. She would get Theo ready and take him down to wait for his bus at 8 a.m. They were lucky to have found a nanny who was a student and who liked a two-hour job each morning before her own school day began then three hours in the late afternoon once her classes were over and Theo arrived home on the bus.

Aimee's introduction to the Brooks family had been fortuitous and random. At a rare dinner party, hosted by one of Jonathan's few remaining friends, Jonathan was seated beside an Irish lawyer, a broad-shouldered, gregarious type, as he spoke about looking for a nanny. The man responded that his nieces in Dublin had a beloved sitter who was heading to New York on a student visa and looking for work as a nanny. Carly had pursued this new option fervently. They'd had numerous sitters in the past but never had help five days a week. Jonathan agreed with Carly; they should have found help much sooner.

Recently, Jonathan had developed a feeling of mild anxiety when Aimee rang the doorbell in the morning or as he turned his key in the lock after returning home at 6:00 p.m. This had to do with his minor confrontations with Aimee, her observation of his parental shortcomings, which apparently swung between over-protection and neglect in her eyes. Aimee was a graduate student in special education and child development.

This fact was part of why he and Carly had wanted her but also part of why Jonathan was uncomfortable with her. He felt scrutinized and at times inferior. Some days, his anxiety hinged on nothing more than her visible boredom with spending five minutes with him while reporting on Theo's day. Never bored with Theo, just unimpressed with the father.

Jonathan let Aimee in, taking in her ever-present ponytail restraining her unruly reddish hair, her upturned nose, and nearly black eyes. She wore her summer uniform of a white t-shirt and cut-off shorts. She was petite in every way—but had the forbearance of a tall woman. She kicked off her sandals and immediately went to where Theo sat by the bookcase. "Good morning, Theo. You have time for one book before we get you out the door for school. How're you, Mr. Brooks?"

"Please call me Jonathan. We're good. How are you?"

"Grand." Aimee was already seated on the couch, urging Theo to crawl over and climb up. Aimee never lifted or carried Theo the way Jonathan sometimes did, unconsciously rushing things along. Jonathan noticed and remembered the faint bruises on Theo's knees as he scooted to Aimee.

"Aimee, Theo has bruises on his knees. Do you know how that happened?"

Aimee smiled strangely, giving Jonathan chills. "Oh yes, we spent the whole afternoon on Friday practicing climbing the front stoop."

"Why would you do that?"

"Are you kidding?" Aimee stood while Theo stalled on the floor, staring up at Aimee's legs. Jonathan observed that Theo was sensing the tension between them but he carried on, unable not to.

"He can't climb stairs," Jonathan said. "We already know

that. It was ninety degrees Friday. The steps are concrete and bruised his legs." Jonathan pointed at Theo, "And we don't need the whole neighborhood observing some ad-hoc PT session for a seven-year-old who can't climb ten steps." He held his empty coffee cup in his hand, feeling outrageously awkward. He wasn't shouting but noticed a violent grip on his heart that felt as if he were.

"Your neighbors? They all know Theo."

"You know what I mean!"

"I don't." Aimee sat again and patted the couch for Theo, "It's okay Theo, come up here. I'm very sorry he has some bruises, but he did climb the steps, and he needs a lot more challenges to learn to do—everything!"

Jonathan sickened seeing that Theo's mouth was crumpling; he was about to cry. Aimee bent over and stroked Theo's shoulder, where he was seated on the floor. It seemed she was hiding her face from Jonathan too.

"I'll go get ready for work." The words "sorry" and "thank you" were on his lips too, but they stuck and didn't come out of his mouth. Which was it? Was he right or wrong? Jonathan left the room with equal parts relief and frustration. Aimee vexed him, and he knew he vexed her, but after three months, he sensed Theo striving harder, maybe wanting to impress Aimee herself or just becoming more driven. Either way, Jonathan suspected it had to do with Aimee. She was motivating Theo, and for that, he was grateful.

He recalled the first time they met. She'd cocked her head at Theo scooting along the floor to meet her in the foyer. She'd said, "hi Theo, it's nice to meet you." She'd squatted and held out one hand. Theo grasped it. And then the two of them locked eyes and took a good long look at each other.

Theo

THE GROUND was hard before but turned to water. My feet fall through and sink, so I learn to swim. I think the floor is still hard for everyone else. Their feet find the hard and walk across it. My feet sink and there is no bottom. I swim and still go where I want.

2.

When Jonathan arrived at work his foreman, Joe Buckner, updated him on the morning's progress. The site was strangely still, as if no one was working. The union construction workers, mostly from Long Island, had arrived at five that morning. Four of the eighteen carpenters were out sick. The remaining workers were capable of installing the water pipes and electrical wires for the next phase of the south-facing offices. But they were idle, touting the infraction that would constitute for the plumbers and electricians' unions.

"And a guy from the state is on sixteen, pacing it out for the number of solar panels."

"The state? There's someone here on the roof? We're not doing any solar on this job."

"Well, he said he's from the Department of Energy, seemed like a real son-of-a-bitch too." The foreman poked Jonathan's ID which was clipped to his shirt pocket, and carried the emblem of the Department of Buildings. "But hey, maybe he's got the wrong address." Buckner seemed to be enjoying himself, shrugging with exaggeration.

"No. This is how it works. State offices never know what their other hand is doing. And just look at the sun all down the Avenue," Jonathan waved his arm toward 5th Avenue and tilted his head back, lifting the brim of his hard hat and squinting, "It's free electricity, about $25,000 a year for a building of this volume. Someone got wise. I'll go see him." As Jonathan walked toward the open-air lift he called, "Tell the guys to take lunch."

"At eight-thirty? They usually take their lunch at nine."

"Let the union stage a protest that lunch was half an hour early. I don't care." Jonathan insisted his workers were unionized and he valued the security and benefits it provided them all, but he often related to his foreman with this mutual gruffness.

As Jonathan bounced up the sixteen floors inside the metal cage, "I don't care," echoed in his head. The truth was he cared a lot. This building could be beautiful. And in New York City many new ones weren't.

Jonathan had argued with a guy at a conference a month earlier around this subject. The man complained that the developers of the early 2000s boom had put up redundant, modern, reflective glass curves all over the city, with no concern for how they fit in with the buildings around them. He said they would ruin the city "forever." Jonathan agreed about the buildings, but had to adjust, "Not forever." To which this man shouted, "Yes—forever!" as though Jonathan himself erected each offending skyscraper. Jonathan thought to explain that every couple hundred years the city would turn-over wholesale, but he didn't like the guy enough to prolong their conversation. How could any adult use the word *forever*? Ever.

Jolting to a stop at the current roofline, Jonathan swung open the short gate to exit the cage. He hooked his safety harness to the crossbar. The solar guy, in orange vest and hard hat was close to the western edge, looking at his feet.

"Hello. Good morning," Jonathan called out so he wouldn't startle the guy on the beams.

Then Jonathan looked at his own feet, as he approached. When he looked up again he was utterly confused. A woman stood before him with her hair tucked into her hard hat. She held up one finger, with her cell phone pressed to her ear.

"Let's discuss it tonight, okay? 9 o'clock?" She listened for the answer and then turned off her cell and dropped it into her vest pocket.

From where Jonathan stood she seemed to float surrounded by blue sky, though she stood firmly on the grated catwalk. Vertigo overcame him, until he shuffled his own feet.

"Hi. You're the Project Manager?" She asked.

Jonathan held out his hand, "Yes, Jonathan Brooks."

"Sara Danner, Department of Energy."

It was exactly Buckman's sense of humor to tell Jonathan that the attractive engineer on the roof was a man. He probably joked to the guys that Jonathan would fall off his beam at the sight of a pretty blonde. It was rare to see a woman on their job sites. At an earlier time in his life, this particular woman would have awakened his flirtatious self. But Jonathan, as Theo's father who was separated from Carly, saw her through a scrim, removed from his reality.

"You're investigating for solar? Has it been executed by the DOE?"

"I'd initiate the execution after my review, but yes–stimulus money comes to New York. At first impression, it's a good location. 11,000 square feet of roof space, right?"

Jonathan looked north. The needles of the Chrysler and the Empire State building popped from the crowded skyline, as they always did for him. His beacons that placed and centered him. His eyes always sought those two skyscrapers, like stars, when he viewed New York's skyline. They'd been rivals in their "race to the sky." Completing just eleven months apart, with the architects of both raising the heights of the original plans, trying to be the tallest. But nearly a hundred years later, Jonathan viewed them as companions. They'd withstood time together, their competition had built mutual respect. Jonathan saw them as living, breathing elder statesmen of New York.

Jonathan answered Sara's question as precisely as he could. "Here on the sixteenth floor it's 11,200. There will be a south-facing executive terrace right here, so the ultimate roof on the 25th will be only 10,600."

Sara smiled at Jonathan's exactitude, which immediately became fuddy-duddy, under her smile.

"Well, I think it's a prime candidate for solar. What do you think?"

A man wouldn't have asked, and it was part of why Jonathan liked women.

"I agree. I could look more closely at the specs for making it a green building." He hadn't done this, but he would do an assessment that night after putting Theo to bed.

"It doesn't take too much right now to submit a bid for stimulus funds and you have to act quickly on these things. I'll work on it this evening. The money could be reverted before the end of the year, but people always hesitate to spend well. We need to grasp the opportunities to do good." Sara Danner was unafraid to sound like an idealist. Jonathan found it refreshing.

"Okay. Let's both look into it. You can send me your initial report." Jonathan handed her a business card. A breeze pressed into him and he slightly bent his knees.

"Of course." Sara pocketed the card and extracted a laser measuring tape from her cargo pants pocket. Jonathan turned back toward the lift. His eyes fell on the stacks of 9-foot two-by-fours resting on the unmade 16th floor terrace. He knew what the men would do after their lunch.

Jonathan stopped himself from reminding her that she had that caller to work things out with at nine. He merely called out his goodbye as he entered the lift.

—

On his way home, Jonathan anxiously remembered he'd have a second encounter with Aimee, Monday being her late day. As he opened the front door, his intuition was immediately validated. Standing six feet tall in the middle of his living room was a royal blue, vinyl padded staircase, leading to nowhere. It was something one might find in a gymnasium or tumbling class or pre-school. Something Jonathan did not like finding in his 1,000-square-foot apartment. He looked glumly at his dislocated furniture, pushed to the walls.

Aimee was talking to Theo in the kitchen and the apartment had the rich smell of something meaty cooking. He placed his file case in the corner and sunk both hands into the third step of the blue staircase. It gave satisfyingly, firm but soft. But what the hell? He would have to return it.

Aimee appeared wearing his apron, the straps tied double around her waist. "We made a brisket. Theo's not cutting onions yet, but he poured the beer over it and sprinkled on the spices. What do you think?" Aimee pointed her chin at the stairs, a dirty dish towel clutched in both hands.

"Same-day delivery? Is this revenge?"

Aimee pushed back loose strands of hair with the back of her wrist. Her hair contained the spectrum of red, blond and brown, naturally fused on one head. "I ordered it on Friday. I wouldn't 'ave after our chat today. But I'm glad it arrived while I'm 'ere to explain."

"How am I supposed to live with this in the middle of my apartment?"

"You think it looks big now, you should 'ave seen it in its packing."

Theo scooted into the room, one leg bent in front of him on the floor, the other knee pointing up to the ceiling. He scooted to the front side of the steps, and tilting onto all fours, climbed up three steps and spun around to sit like a kid on the bleachers at a ballgame. He was more adept than Jonathan had ever seen.

Jonathan took two strides to reach his boy, and cupped Theo's face in his hands, "Sweetie, how'd you hop right up there?" Theo's eyes danced. "The-eo dun, Dada."

"Theo *did* it–not done it," Aimee corrected. "There's no stairs in your apartment, Mr. Brooks. You were right that the stoop is not appropriate, but he needs steps to learn how to master steps. The YMCA will accept it as a donation when he's mastered them."

"So, I'm a philanthropist. To what tune exactly?"

"What?"

"What did they cost?"

Aimee frowned. "You're so uncool. It's $700, on my credit card. And I need reimbursement before the bill is due. It's way beyond my income."

He took a breath and relaxed his jaw muscles. "Your brisket smells delicious. You've made my son into a mountain climber who pours beer, and you've only temporarily wrecked my place.

I'll fork over the exorbitant fee. But next time let's discuss his therapies and my spending beforehand. Okay?"

"Aye. I hope you realize I'm trying to help Theo."

Jonathan looked at Aimee a long moment, and like a magician's trick, saw himself in her eyes. A reversal of blame. "I can see that. Thank you, Aimee."

"You're welcome."

"And please stop calling me Mr. Brooks!" With Theo riding on his back, Jonathan walked Aimee to the door.

"Oh, by the way," he said, "He loves the Pink Posey you put on him. Said it first thing this morning."

"What's that?"

"I assumed the nail polish."

Halfway out the door, Aimee picked up Theo's foot and stroked one tiny painted toenail with her thumb.

"I don't know the name. But glad you like something else I did." She left without repeating her goodbyes.

Theo

BUILDING IS on papers Dada see. His phone is building. His talk is building. He look at me. But he *see* building.

Mee-Mee come from far away. Her voice new song. Mee-Mee *see* me. No sad in her eyes.

Dada is mad that I swim now instead of walk. Aimee tries to make hard spots I can stand on. It doesn't work, but I like to try with her. One day Aimee try to move like me. She swam all over floor with me. She chased me and I was much faster. But I laughed so much she caught me. She said, "Theo, you're a smart kid. That's a fast way to move around."

3.

AIMEE'S FAMILY owned a small dairy farm in County Kerry with sixty head of cattle. Small enough that Aimee's father and her four older brothers could handle all the milking, mucking of stalls, feeding and general care of their forty Stiltons. Just large enough that they all ate, had school uniforms, new almost every year, and cable television.

Despite her regular state of inebriation, Pauline managed the farm's books, could attend a heifer in labor, bake soda bread, wash and iron sheets, do basic carpentry, sew, and do fine embroidery. Aimee watched her mother do everything. Pauline loved having a daughter after so many boys. She added bits of lace to almost everything Aimee wore, from her night-gown hems to her school-blouse pockets, to her apron and pink washcloths and towels.

Aimee had a mane of hair that was strawberry, blond and brown all at once, that always hung loose down her back and ended in a tangle of curls. Pauline would methodically stroke her daughter's hair at night in front of the TV, between sips of gin.

Aimee loved her mum without question, but she found her attentions suffocating. Between the late-life pregnancy and the heavy drinking, Pauline never lost her final baby weight and looked six months pregnant forevermore. She made embarrassing, non-sequitur comments and she laughed too hard after her own jokes, often leaving spit on the person's face she was speaking to. Pauline was a clumsy drunk who knocked things over or toppled herself.

After the animals were attended to, Jack O'Malley and Aimee's four older brothers came indoors for a family dinner. After eating they watched a different TV set in a different room from Pauline and Aimee. Aimee kissed her mother goodnight before Pauline would pass-out on the couch, and she often found her mother rubbing her eyes awake in the same clothes on the couch in the early morning. Thus, it was Aimee who discovered her mother had died during the night.

Standing beside her deceased mother at dawn, seven-year-old Aimee took several moments to add together what she knew of this strange story that was her life. Her mother was forty-three when she conceived her, a 'change-of-life baby,' her mum had told her. And she was a well-known drinker. No one, from neighbor to church member, to her dad or brothers, had seen Pauline sober in recent years. Mum became Pauline as Aimee stood there, writing her own young biography. Her mother had a sweet sickly smell, in life and death. She had often stumbled sideways while carrying her groceries or a milk pail and was prone to either belligerent outbursts or amorous attacks.

The story Aimee knew was that when the doctor called Dad with Pauline's test results, he'd said, "Are you sitting down, Jack? I think I might have some very surprising news for you. Pauline's expecting a baby, about six months along already."

"A baby?" Shouted Pauline O'Malley. "Don't know how I thought all these little kicks were indigestion. Must be losing it. What'd he call *you* for? Chauvinist."

"Paulie, you have to quit drinking now, you know."

"Sure I do. Can't be going on the lash with a lil' one on board. If God put another soul in me at this age, he's got plans for it."

Pauline did quit drinking for a week. But one week was all her system could handle. At first just one drink and then four the next day, and ten days after her visit to the doctor, she was drunk as ever, getting around town with her growing belly.

When Pauline went to the hospital in labor, smelling like warm gin and shouting at every person that touched her, the doctor felt compelled to warn Jack that the baby might be weak of heart, underweight and alcohol-affected, might just not make it, he'd gone so far so say.

Jack responded, "Pauline's God will be the judge of that."

Aimee had been told multiple times by Pauline that she was "a perfect six-pound bundle." She'd passed every exam with flying colors. Aimee had no idea what exams they gave to newborns. When she was wrapped in a tight swaddle and pink cap, and placed in her Mum's arms, Pauline said to Jack, "We got our lass. She was determined."

Both her parents had told her that at ten months of age, she began to walk on skinny, bowed legs. Pauline said she had looked around her crib with a critical eye from her first weeks and undid her swaddle to flip over by a month. "You joined me doing chores by age two, sweeping the floor with your own short broom and putting up toys, shoes, newspapers, anything left about." Her dad added, "You could lead the cows into the barn at two and a half."

Aimee buried her nose in her mother's neck and cried before alerting Dad that Pauline had passed.

As she outgrew her clothes, Aimee's wardrobe gradually became free of lace. She realized the lace-trimmed garments were slowly dwindling and she began to think of them as her own feelings of mourning, reducing and disappearing over time, a naturally occurring event. Until one day her life would be without mourning and grief and without feminine decoration.

Aimee began doing the same farm chores as her brothers and watched news or sports with them at night on the same television. Life was happier and easier having joined the stronger ranks of the O'Malley family.

Aimee was fourteen when she had her first boyfriend. Connor Dillon worked in town at the one delicatessen, behind the meat counter. He was six feet tall, handsome, gentle and eighteen years old. Their four-year age difference didn't matter because Aimee was frighteningly self-knowing and mature and Connor was simple. He loved American football, comic books, riding his motorcycle, and Aimee.

Their relationship consisted of canoeing on the tiny lake behind Connor's house checking the raw-chicken-baited turtle traps, seeing movies, weekend drives in Connor's jeep, and Saturday lunches at the delicatessen.

Like her mother, then deceased exactly as long as she had been in Aimee's life, Connor loved to stroke the long reddish-blond curls that hung down Aimee's back. And as with her mother, Aimee tolerated this affection without complaint. She herself enjoyed running her fingers through their horse's tail in the barn, after currying and washing his coat. However, she could not see why a person would have the urge to treat another person like a horse's tail.

With calculation, Aimee decided that on the weekend after Connor's graduation from Secondary School, she would lose her virginity and her boyfriend in one culminating event. She wanted to get the sexual act accomplished, and she knew the match wasn't really a well-suited one, nor would she enter the one Secondary School that fall as a freshman with a full-grown boyfriend. Every teen in their county was known to one another and there was no one who didn't know that Connor and Aimee were a couple, but she was already familiar with the short memories that her peers were endowed with. She knew if she ended her year-long relationship with Connor at the beginning of the summer and was known only as an unattached girl who swam at Friar's Pond, shopped at the general store, and used the computers at the library all summer, that by fall of her freshman year she'd no longer be Connor's girl.

Although they'd never had sex, for months Connor had perfected how to give Aimee an orgasm with his fingers and he leapt to perform the achievement whenever given the opportunity. Aimee and Connor made-out and groped each other beneath t-shirts and jeans several times a week, whenever they were together, and although she was clear-eyed on it being time to leave the confines of the boyfriend-girlfriend relationship, Aimee knew she would miss him and that she would miss the kissing and touching. She wasn't just trying to discard her virginity, she had gotten pretty hot to experience sex, something she'd witnessed between farm animals, which she assumed was partially the same thing, although she planned on doing it face-to-face.

On a Saturday night in Connor's bedroom, when he reached his hand into the top of her panties, no longer lacey, but black cotton, Aimee grasped his hand and said, "Let's really do it, I'm ready." She hoped she'd have an orgasm from intercourse and thought it best to divert their usual activity that way. Connor grinned and looked as handsome as she'd ever seen him, his face already golden from the spring sun, his fair hair falling in his eyes. Connor had a condom and enjoyed introducing Aimee to the "little hat" and how you saw that it was the right side, and how to pinch the tip and roll it down all the way. In fact, she felt so close to him then that she wondered why they wouldn't keep at it, why she would end it after just one time. But for Aimee it was as inevitable as letting Connor inside her was.

"Are you serious?" was Connor's reaction, twenty minutes after they'd had sex, Connor having total abandon and perhaps even crying when he came, and then making sure Aimee came to orgasm in the usual way afterwards when she was unable to during intercourse. She could only nod, she suddenly felt so upset. "But for what reason? And why did you just do that?"

She had no answers and turned away, in tears. Aimee thought for the first time then that she was going to be leaving Ireland–and that somehow seemed part of the why. But she didn't utter those words to Connor, feeling frankly silly. Aimee was distraught and must have been frustratingly impossible to understand for the next hour they stayed together in Connor's room.

The next day she felt almost normal and that she'd done what was needed. After completing her chores and some of her brother's even, she called Connor, hoping to begin a new friendship, but he wouldn't speak to her. A week later they both went to the movies with a group of kids, mostly new graduates and a few of her girlfriends who were second-year students. Everyone knew that Connor and Aimee were over, and they sat apart in the theater. Afterwards she laughed in the parking lot with her girlfriends, but as she watched him walk alone to his jeep, she felt miserable and guilty. She would have rather ridden home with Connor, as before, than in a car full of friends. Yet still, Aimee felt she'd accomplished something she needed, and was ready to enter Secondary School by fall.

Aimee moved to Dublin for college and discovered in her dorm-mates and in the handful of college boyfriends she dated, that many more people than she could understand had a tendency to stroke her hair during ordinary conversation and while lying in bed post-coital alike. She loved Dublin and college and readily traded her tall wellies for black-leather motorcycle boots, traded the smell of urine-soaked hay for taxi and bus exhaust, the taste of raw milk for the taste of pints of lager (although always with the caution of an adult child of an alcoholic). Aimee traded the country for the city, and her expert knowledge of running a farm for her initially very rudimentary knowledge of Child Psychology.

When Aimee graduated four years later, she immediately applied to graduate programs in New York City in Child Psychology and Early Childhood Education. Before leaving Dublin with her student visa and carry-on suitcase, she had secured a job working for a single dad named Jonathan Brooks, who had "one young son with several disabilities," an email that had made her narrow her eyes and scowl before she'd even met Mr. Brooks.

The day before moving to America, Aimee saw a barber who un-ceremoniously lopped off her ponytail, leaving her hair somewhere between chin and shoulders, a length of loose curls that no one would consider it their innate right to stroke.

4.

JONATHAN LIFTED the brisket out of the roasting pan with two large serving forks and lowered it onto a moated cutting board. It was dressed in translucent onions and whole peppercorns and had a delicious meaty aroma. He wondered if Aimee was a cook in general or if this was her one specialty. He was grateful either way. Jonathan had long-ago grown accustomed to being the only cook in the house. He'd enjoyed cooking since his grad school days and still enjoyed making a nice meal. But it was a rare treat to come home to dinner prepared by someone else. And this night presented a double treat. Theo had shocked him by climbing up a set of stairs in a manner he hadn't known possible. Aimee was now peaceably gone. And he was ready to sit down to a sumptuous meal with his son.

On Theo's dinner plate he placed two slices of tender brisket and then cut them into bites. He made sure there were no onions or peppercorns on his plate. He then placed three hunks of potatoes from the same pot, on the plate, and lastly some crunchy salad on the side. The way Theo liked it—just romaine hearts with vinaigrette.

He laid his own plate with four slices of brisket, lots of onions and peppercorns, and heaping with potatoes and salad. He poured himself a glass of white wine.

He carried the two plates from kitchen to the dining table in one corner of the living room.

"Theo, come eat the beautiful dinner you made tonight!"

Theo looked up from his blocks. He smiled brightly and yelled, "No!" Theo began scooting to the table. "Mee-Mee cook."

"Didn't you help her?" Jonathan poured milk into a small cup for Theo.

"No. I cook."

There were times when Theo prefaced every statement with no. Jonathan could see that this night might be one of them. He tested it out.

"Were you playing with your blocks?"

"No. I play slyspacer." Theo reached his Stokke chair and pushed the footstool against the base of it. Putting one knee on the footstool and grasping the untippable chair, allowed him to climb into the chair unassisted. Jonathan watched, noting that the way he climbed the stool and chair was pretty close to the way he'd climbed up Aimee's staircase.

"Skyscraper. You're doing great, Theo."

"No."

Theo sat and started eating the pieces of meat immediately with his fork.

"Well I think you are."

Jonathan and Theo ate for several minutes without talking. Halfway through his meal, he remembered his wine. After taking a long sip, he leaned back and slowed down to enjoy the food and the time more. He often felt the need to complete things at home, even when he was in a perfectly good mood. He was currently in a very good mood he realized. Theo's accomplishment, the restored equanimity with Aimee, the pending lunch date with Sara Danner from the Department of Energy. He drank more wine.

"Theo, do you like that staircase? Is it fun to climb?"

"No." He was chasing a chunk of potato with his toddler fork. It slipped around his plate evading the blunt tongs of his tool.

"I think you liked climbing up all by yourself. Almost all the way to the top."

Theo didn't bother acknowledging his father's pointless comments. Jonathan knew that expressing too much excitement about any achievement caused Theo to shy away from the accomplishment. And he was a Zen master at staying in the present.

"Can you get that potato with your fork?"

"Yes." This was still contrariness.

After dinner, Jonathan pushed the couch and his Saarinen armchair into new positions to accommodate the staircase, but so that the area still resembled their living room. He read for half an hour in the armchair while Theo sat on the rug pushing plastic colored pegs into a plastic board. Without realizing he'd laid down his newspaper, he noted the design of the toy as if for the first time. Had he bought it? He couldn't recall. Behind the clear plastic board, attached one of five colorful forms–a butterfly, a ship, etc. The child was supposed to insert the colored pegs that corresponded with the picture. To his surprise, Theo was placing the right color pegs over the caterpillar pattern before him, green body, blue feet, red antennae.

"What color is that, Boomer?" He interrupted Theo's concentration, and he stared at Jonathan, seemingly totally unaware of the yellow peg gripped in his fingers. Jonathan knew Theo wouldn't say the color. The task of placing the right color peg in the corresponding hole was one brain function, and not related to verbalizing a name for an object or utilizing language identification. Theo looked at Jonathan, because he'd spoken to him, but no reply was forthcoming. He stopped what he was doing and just sat smiling, in fact his body grew inert where before it was active. Jonathan regretted breaking Theo's action. He let the newspaper fall to the floor and he dove down beside his boy to hug him around the waist and bring his attention back to the toy.

"Are you making a caterpillar? You're doing a great job." He tickled Theo for a moment and Theo twisted from side-to-side, squirming and giggling. When he stopped, Theo put his hand to his dad's waist and piano-ed his fingertips, his smile huge and wet.

"Oh, you're tickling Daddy now!"

Theo was beautiful, with dark blond curls that turned slightly green from chlorine if he did lots of swimming therapy, and green eyes which he'd gotten from him. Jonathan was privately glad he had this one advantage in life. His beautiful boy.

"Do one more peg and then we better go take a bath and get ready for bed." To Jonathan's happy surprise, Theo put down the yellow and picked up a red, popping it into the caterpillar's red antennae.

"Cat pillar."

Jonathan beamed, "You. Amaze. Me."

—

After getting Theo to bed, Jonathan poured a cold glass of wine and wished he could pour Carly one too. He felt the urge for a toast to Theo. Instead of letting the thought depress him, he reached for his phone.

Carly picked up on the second ring. "Is everything okay?"

"Hi, Jonathan, how are you? Nice to hear from you." He modeled cheerfully.

"Sure, all that. I was surprised to see your call."

"Everything's quite okay–good even."

"Everything? That's a good feeling."

Jonathan could hear her smile. "I want to tell you what Theo did today. Aimee bought a contraption, a foam staircase– that's a whole other story, but she taught Theo to climb it. When I got home from work, Theo hopped up it, turned around and sat down facing me, very dexterously. He was so proud of himself." Jonathan was reliving the sight of their strong boy, his straight posture on the staircase.

Carly was silent a moment. "How many stairs?"

"Three." Jonathan felt a twinge of annoyance.

"On his feet?"

I don't know—No, not on his feet, on his hands and knees."

"He's been able to do that for a couple of months. That was in his last assessment, that he could climb several stairs."

Although Theo slept at his house eighty percent of the time, it was Carly who managed his therapy appointments still—all during weekdays while Jonathan worked. Carly arranged her freelance schedule around Theo's many therapies and coordinated with Aimee to get him there. Carly gave Jonathan copies of every assessment, long litanies of skills being acquired: using utensils, taking off coat and shoes, stacking, pouring, sorting, sitting upright without support, and perhaps—climbing stairs. Jonathan's problem was he only believed what he saw with his own eyes. He'd never seen Theo climb a few stairs. An emotion washed over him that held the whole sad fact of Theo's seven-year struggle, how small and non-transferable this accomplishment was, what had happened to him and Carly as a couple and to their individual personalities, something that felt like a death.

"Aimee's been a great nanny for Theo. Now he can practice stairs daily at home."

Jonathan and Carly had a routine. They alternated their optimism and hopelessness and played counter to each other as some form of support, or just perpetual motion.

"Yeah, let's keep pushing him. Let's not accept the status quo that he's done progressing and we're just keeping him clean." Jonathan cringed as he heard himself speak, but he felt as tied to his remark as an actor to his script.

Carly made a small noise in her throat, *hnn,* and Jonathan felt the unfairness of his call. They remained separated, neither had found any motivation to get divorced, and this way his employer health insurance still covered the whole family. But being separated had some rules that they'd discovered rather than made. And one of those rules was you couldn't ruin each other's Friday nights with your irrational moods. That was for married people.

"I'm onboard, Jonathan. Nothing has slacked off for him, ever. I'll tell his physical therapist about the new stairs on Monday." Carly took a deep breath. "I should get going, unless there's something else?"

"Yeah. I actually have work to get to. Some code related stuff for the Jetson." He feared their early courtship was alluded to in this utterance too. On one of their first dates, Jonathan had grown very animated describing his deep passion for the New York City skyscraper and the sociological and technological intersections that built the city. Carly had responded with the kind of shared enthusiasm that built new relationships. By referring to the Jetson, Jonathan revealed to himself all the baggage that came along with everything related to Carly.

"Well, goodnight then."

There was never one clear feeling when it came to Carly. Their love and history a muddled mess—a tar pit that held all the fossilized evidence but could never be sorted.

Jonathan rallied himself with the image of Sara, the Department of Energy engineer, standing on the beams, the wind lifting pieces of her hair, hoping to save his evening from a sour mood, he turned to work.

Jonathan got online and re-read Green Building Law and Local Law 86. Opening a new window, he read the requirements for city-owned and city-funded green buildings. The Jetson was privately owned by the developer, but partially city-funded and federally-funded, as almost anything that began during the stimulus was. Good luck America, Jonathan projected without sarcasm. He popped around the Internet re-reading standards for green buildings and recent findings and decisions from the committee on housing and buildings.

The Jetson was not pre-determined to be a green building. If Sara Danner had worked for the Department of Energy for more than a few months she knew how unlikely this designation was. These things were decided before ground was ever broken, and the chances of him, or anyone, especially this developer, improbably named Browncage, pursuing the tough environmental regulations for a luxury residential/commercial skyscraper were close to null. Still Jonathan felt like cultivating his green talking points for his next conversation with the woman he'd met thirty-five stories in the air. And perhaps there were smaller green choices they, *he* could make as the Jetson was erected.

It occurred to Jonathan that Carly might have had company. Or was she heading out? Did she have plans? She was after-all an adult without a kid in bed. He had an underlying assumption that

Carly wasn't lonely in their separation. For her it was a choice, something added. For him it was an absence. But several years in, it had grown to feel mutually desired, or at least mutually accepted as necessary. Yet, he never felt he was quite succeeding with being single.

He opened another window and went into his account with Pullman's Supplies. His recent purchases were all visible at a glance, as well as the smart website's anticipated needs for each customer. He was ready to order lintels, soft flooring, and additional plumbing, and before clicking his usual brands and materials, he scrolled the sustainable options. He read that Unibond Flex Platinum was an NSF-140 platinum certified sheet carpet backing that contained no PVC, no 4PCH or SBR latex.

Jonathan had read extensively on the harmful effects of chemicals used in construction materials. And he knew men, many men, and a few women, who had cancer from working on the pile in the days and weeks immediately after 9/11.

He believed that these chemical pours, including the flame retardant that was on almost all furniture, and even on children's pajamas and mattresses, caused harm. Toxins were everywhere. All American women had toxins in their breast milk. Umbilical cords even held trace amounts of the chemicals we lived with.

He paused to consider what had harmed Theo, what had made him sick. It would remain an unknown for the rest of their lives why Theo got encephalitis. And why he didn't fully recover from it.

Theo was physically and verbally far behind. But what else were they sure of? Very little. Dr. Wyatt believed he did not have cognitive delays. Which meant in short that Theo's intelligence was unharmed.

Jonathan remembered visiting the Bronx Zoo with Theo last summer. They'd huddled on their side of the glass where they had long, sustained eye contact with a female gorilla. She leaned the side of her massive body against the glass and stared into Jonathan's eyes. Eventually the gorilla raised her hand and pressed her palm to the glass. Jonathan placed his opposite palm against hers, lining up the five digits with hers. With his free hand he wiped away his sudden tears. *What was this intelligent creature doing here? Why was she caged to return the gaze of curious humans all day?*

Jonathan could perceive the gorilla's intelligence without any doubt. And he perceived Theo's even more clearly. Theo was not cognitively disabled. He was intelligent and stuck with a body he couldn't control and speech he couldn't utter.

Jonathan added the non-toxic carpet backing to his accounts cart, costing Browncage ten percent more on one item in one order out of probably seventy-five orders placed during the three years of construction. A small drop in the bucket, but a choice that gave Jonathan satisfaction. The building would be cleaner by some degree. He blushed knowing he would tell Sara Danner he'd done this inconsequential thing. He wouldn't complete the purchase until Monday anyway. As he closed his laptop, he thought that Sara might be on her call right now with who he guessed was a disgruntled lover. Without meaning to he'd noticed and remembered the way she'd ended a call as he approached her. The curt intimacy. He had already imagined it was a new boyfriend who felt he was never prioritized.

—

The next morning, Jonathan made a rare decision to take Theo to brunch. He disliked this pastime on numerous levels.

The waiters were rushed, the cooks at half-attention, and the restaurants were cramped and diners generally cranky. Children and brunch were diametrically opposed, thought Jonathan, and brunch in a restaurant with Theo was especially without merits. But that Saturday, the weather was end-of-summer glorious. Jonathan felt that even if Theo had climbed stairs before, what he witnessed the day before deserved some form of celebration. And because he'd stayed up late drinking wine, Jonathan was hungry again at ten-thirty, craving something richer than their seven a.m. Cheerios. As he hurried them both into their clothes, the morning felt reminiscent of his younger years when, slightly hung-over on Saturdays and Sundays, he and Carly frequently went to brunch with their other childless friends.

The day was beautiful. As they crossed Smith Street to walk on the sunny side, Jonathan caught the long gaze of a woman crossing the other way. Her eyes were not on him but lingering on Theo. Theo was sitting in a large jogger stroller, sturdy and big enough to carry a fifty-pound boy. He was often aware that Theo passed for a typical New York City kid, wheeling around the city well into childhood for speed and efficiency. But other times he caught people's eyes, women's almost always, lingering on Theo's inert posture, or the inward collapse of his knees, and then registering the stroller wasn't normal for a child this age, nor was the child himself "normal." At the last moment, Jonathan said "Good morning" to this passing woman, determined to just enjoy this walk down the street.

He chose Cafe Luluc on Smith Street because it had high-backed booths that Theo could sit in comfortably without any additional supports, and because they had excellent eggs Benedict as well as scrambled eggs and skinny French fries for Theo. Many people, like Jonathan, waited outside for the place to open, so it seemed the restaurant could fill entirely in five minutes. Outside with the small crowd, Theo fretted with his harness, wanting to be put on the sidewalk, free to scoot. "One second, sweetie. They're about to open." Jonathan strategized as usual about how he'd bring Theo in. Maneuvering the stroller through the front door with such a big kid in it was conspicuous; carrying him was worse. Theo scooting in on his butt with one foot propelling him was out of the question.

One day, Theo might propel himself into restaurants in an electric wheelchair. Jonathan simultaneously longed for and rebelled against that reality. After Theo's second birthday and his comprehensive evaluation, that had led to a full regimen of therapies, Carly had texted Jonathan a fifteen-second video of Theo seated in a wheelchair, huge Velcro straps around his chest and waist. Theo's hand hovered above the joystick as though it were a hot stove he shouldn't touch. In the last three seconds of the video, Theo bumped the joystick and the chair bucked forward. Theo shrieked in surprise and then cried.

When Jonathan received that video unexpectedly, he'd shuddered, every part of him rejecting that possibility. Six months earlier, Theo could run. Had someone decided, someone with power over their future, that Theo would never walk again?

"What?" He'd texted Carly. His hands shaking.

"He gets to try it out once a month in physical therapy. It's a long time before he'd get one."

Jonathan wrote and deleted three different responses. He was sitting at his desk at work, the same desk he'd sat behind six months earlier when Carly called and said Theo had a fever. Was it over now? Had they lost the battle?

Eventually he wrote Carly back, just, "He's a champ." Jonathan didn't want to argue with Carly anymore. He didn't want his heart to ache anymore.

Finally, the restaurant's front door was propped open. Jonathan concentrated on the idea of a bowl-sized cappuccino and a mimosa as he swiftly strolled in, lifted Theo out of the stroller and into the booth, and quickly ran the un-foldable stroller back out to the sidewalk. When he returned, Theo slapped the table top with two palms and cheered, "Daddy!"

"That's me, Sunshine."

The waiter, who miraculously seemed to remember them from an entire year ago, brought menus immediately, and took their drink order, a mimosa and a coffee for Jonathan, and an orange juice for Theo.

A moment later, Jonathan raised his Champagne flute to Theo and he raised his tiny orange juice cup. "To being memorable," he said.

Theo clinked his glass, a trick he'd picked up around age two, that Jonathan and Carly had definitely not taught him. *New York*, he thought.

"Br-unch men-u." Theo pushed the words from his mouth heavily and then smiled proudly.

Jonathan found this utterance to be wondrous.

"Let's celebrate, Kiddo. Theo want eggs and French fries?" Jonathan caught that, as he frequently did, he'd spoken in poor grammar to his son. He mentally asked himself to stop. "Would you like eggs and fries?"

"Jacks." Theo stated definitively, ignoring Jonathan's question about the food.

"I'll get you scrambled eggs and fries." Jonathan wished they'd have a real conversation. He tried to imagine it for a second. Talk of baseball, of school, trading of corny jokes.

Theo repeated, *"Jacks."* With flat palms on top of his menu, he shifted the menu back and forth as though it were dancing.

The restaurant filled up around them. As they waited for their food, Jonathan took in the bustling scene. Louis Armstrong played from speakers overhead. He enjoyed that this was their neighborhood, their restaurant, their city, and he and Theo belonged out in public, eating a sixty-dollar breakfast for the sake of enjoyment and stimulation, and urban life.

Theo was well-supported in the high-backed red booth they were seated in. But he was restless and grabby. He seemed intent on spilling something. Jonathan took the large sugar jar out of Theo's hand and preventatively moved the salt and pepper and his water glass out of his reach.

Their food arrived. Jonathan busied himself with peppering his eggs, sipping his cappuccino, chewing a fry, all while talking to Theo, an imitation of a real conversation. "We could go to the farmer's market after breakfast. Taste all the pickle samples. Remember the pickle guy?"

Theo interrupted him, rocking the table with his full weight and wearing a wide-eyed expression. He was suddenly butt up in the air, standing on the bench, trying to get away from his wet sweatpants. Right away Jonathan realized his mistake. He'd dressed Theo in underwear and gray sweats. Not only did he forget to use a pull-up, the only safe bet for dining out, but he hadn't taken Theo to the bathroom before leaving the house.

"Shoot! Can you make it to the potty?" Jonathan squeezed around the table. He pictured the narrow passage past the kitchen and the two unisex bathrooms in the back and knew there'd be people waiting their turn in the tiny space. It was almost better that Theo hadn't "made it," which he could now clearly see was the case. Theo crouched, bent forward on the table for support. His pants were soaked, a broad circle of dark gray around his crotch, the entire butt soaked, plush cotton doing nothing to help him.

"I tell you!" Theo shrieked at Jonathan.

Jonathan felt eyes boring into them. His mind raced. If only he'd already paid, he could just scoop Theo up and leave. Theo shrieked again and lifted his eyes from his wet lap to glare at Jonathan, seeking help.

Jonathan lifted his boy from the booth, with a passing disgust, he placed Theo's wet crotch against his own waist. He'd carried him this way forever, what did a little urine matter?

"It's okay, sweetheart. Accidents happen. We'll go home and change."

Theo's pants soaked the side of his dress shirt thoroughly. Jonathan carried him to the bar and asked for a towel, "for an accident." He hoped the bartender thought coffee or water. Jonathan meticulously cleaned the booth, while holding Theo against his hip. He heard the restaurant return to normalcy. But he knew the diners were intentionally looking away, trying to ignore the scene he and Theo were making. He knew they were wondering why this older child wasn't toilet-trained and was being carried like a baby. Jonathan consoled himself that Theo was fairly potty-trained—no small accomplishment—and this was just a series of errors, all on his part.

Jonathan waited by the entrance for an interminable amount of time while they prepared his check, ran his credit card and finally returned his card in exchange for his signature. The entire time, Theo clasped his legs around Jonathan's waist and watched, a little too content with the situation, Jonathan thought. The waiter kindly wrapped up their meals to go, without Jonathan having asked for them.

It occurred to him that he was holding Theo this whole time, something he was loathe to do upon their arrival. The alternative was to put him in the stroller on the sidewalk for several minutes alone, while he ran back in to pay. He wasn't going to leave his boy, who couldn't communicate out on the street that was thronged with Brooklynites enjoying an end-of-summer Sunday.

"We're almost home," he said, to both of them.

—

Mopping the bathroom floor that evening, Jonathan raked lost items out from behind the toilet. He lifted a bottle of lustrous pink nail polish. It was strangely appealing in its triangular glass rocket ship, the white towering cap and hidden wand. Jonathan cleaned the bottle under the tap and then turned it in his hand, thinking of various styles of architecture, Beaux Arts, the Eiffel Tower—nail polish takes its design from architecture, and like good architecture its design is based on function. The elongated cap accommodates the wand and brush.

Turning the bottle upside down, he read the white sticker planted on the bottom, "Pink Posey." His scalp tingled with familiarity.

Jonathan leaned the mop against the bathroom wall and opened the nail polish. Skimming the brush against the lip of the bottle, he painted one stroke of bright pink across his left thumb nail. He brought his nail to his nostrils and inhaled deeply. Overcome with dizziness he leaned against the wall and shut his eyes. Just as quickly they popped open. *Brunch Menu.*

Was it possible?

Jonathan quickly resealed the nail polish and strode from the room directly to Theo's room, where he was playing on the floor. Jonathan looked at his boy lining up lettered blocks, an animal atop each one, a destination-less parade. He looked at the nail polish bottle resting in his palm. There's no way. But the pre-dawn morning ten days earlier crystalized in his memory. Theo had shown him his toes and said those two words. Aimee didn't even know the name.

Jonathan kneeled beside Theo and held out the bottle upside down.

"Honey, what does this say?"

Theo reached for it. He touched one finger to the sticker adhered to the bottom. "Pink Posey."

Jonathan frantically looked around the room for something with words on it. He lunged for Theo's bookshelf and searched for a book with a simple title. "Hug." They'd read that for years. He yanked it.

"What's this say?"

"Hug."

He was articulating better than usual. Guided by the letters? This was not a good test, his reeling mind told him. He'd read Theo this book hundreds of times; he would know the title by heart. Jonathan stood and started to walk from the room in search of a document Theo had never seen before. When Theo was much younger Jonathan and Carly used to support him under his arms and walk him about, bearing all his weight, but teaching him the feel of walking upright, so they thought. Eventually their physical therapist told them to stop. His brain and leg muscles weren't communicating. He wasn't learning anything. He was being dragged and would be better off maneuvering by his own means, however it occurred. Jonathan stopped in Theo's doorway.

"Wanna walk with Daddy?"

He came back to his boy and scooped his body up from behind, holding him around his chest. Theo was on his feet, but fully in Jonathan's arms, his legs dangling. Theo was so much taller than the last time they'd done this. Feeling out of control, he walked his son to the living room. Theo laughed through it all, horseplay to him. In the living room Jonathan settled Theo on his practice staircase, and he reached for a magazine.

He turned the pages arbitrarily. What was he looking for? It felt like roulette. If he chose the right words, the right font size, color, simplicity, Theo might read it. But he had to bet well. He found a dark photograph of New York's skyline. He'd enjoyed this piece on city planning during the New Deal era. Across the top of the photo in large white print were the words, "The City." Jonathan sat on the second step beside Theo. With shaking hands, he held out the magazine, folded open and facing him, like a platter of treats for him to choose from.

"What does this say, honey?"

"The city."

Jonathan's mouth fell open as he exhaled a giant breath, "Haa," Theo repeated, "Haa."

"You can read, Theo Brooks. Who are you?"

Jonathan gave Theo the magazine and covered his face. He shook uncontrollably. His mind raced everywhere from what they would do now, to what they hadn't been doing, to what the possibilities were. For the first time in years he pictured Theo with a future he could understand. Theo returned. He pictured his beautiful son going to college in a wheelchair. For years he forbade any fantasies or images. He simultaneously wept for the sheer possibility and for what he still suspected were unattainable dreams. He wept with self-hatred for having slowed to a halt. He realized just how much they'd slowed down. He deserved Aimee's harsh criticism. Because she didn't know him before, she knew only the Jonathan he'd become. A Jonathan who had accepted everything wholesale and gotten on with it. Someone who had given up.

"I'm sorry, Theo. I couldn't be more sorry."

Theo

WHEN WE go out, Mee-Mee say, "You have to visit the *jacks*, Theo? Let's go try."

And home Mee-Mee say too, "Use the *jacks,* Theo."

I tell Dada, *"Jacks!"* But he thinking something, not listening to me.

Mee-Mee and Mommy know what to do more.

Dada carries me when he doesn't want me to swim. I'm not a baby, I just swim instead of walk. Woman stares at me for being carried. It okay. I stare at her too.

I understand words I can see. Letters go together like a family and make a word. But words can't fly from out my mouth like other people do. My words hop out like baby birds who can't fly.

Animals have no words fly out too, only sounds. Maybe they read like me.

5.

ON MONDAY morning, Jonathan and Theo sat on the couch reading. Jonathan had pulled out all of Theo's board books that still remained. Small colorful rounded books, with a few sentences per page. Jonathan slowly turned the pages. Theo read to him.

He felt caught in the act when they heard the doorbell.

Theo leaned forward and peered at him, squealing, "Mee-Mee!"

Jonathan collected the pile of books from his lap, and stood to return them to Theo's room, before buzzing Aimee in. He knew Theo wouldn't mention what they were doing. He lived in the present, rarely speaking of even five minutes in the past or future. Jonathan didn't want to tell Aimee about the reading discovery, not before telling Carly. But he didn't want to tell Carly yet either. Perhaps it was the stairs and how she'd already known. He told himself he could enjoy this discovery all to himself, just for a day or two, before sharing. Sharing would make it less special, and more of a new regimen, rather than just a pleasure to enjoy.

It was like watching the sun rise he thought as he buzzed in Aimee and waited for her to climb the stairs. He wanted to view it, take it in, soak up the natural beauty of his boy and his new gift. He wanted to watch a sunrise as nothing more than a gorgeous and routine act of nature, and not as a sign that it's time to begin another day, time to get to work.

"Good morning." Aimee removed her shoes before entering the apartment.

"Mee-Mee, play with me." Theo called from the couch.

"I want to play with you. Here I come."

Jonathan knew that Aimee would make small rewards of play time in between getting Theo through his morning routine, brushing his teeth, getting dressed, putting on socks and then shoes, alternated with a few puzzle pieces being put together, or a game of Simon Says.

He watched them momentarily, stretching his arms overhead. It was only seven a.m. He hadn't showered yet. He spontaneously decided he would take a run. Five minutes later he was out the door in grey sweatpants and a white t-shirt. Jogging from his Cobble Hill apartment to the Brooklyn Heights promenade, weaving around morning commuters on the sidewalks. He ran four miles easily whenever he allowed himself the time, whether it had been a couple days or a couple of months. Jonathan had run track in high school in the Westchester town he'd grown up in, twenty miles north of New York City. As he ran, he deeply inhaled the perfectly cool air. He often thought of family when he ran.

His older sister, Emily, was his best friend, especially since the separation. Emily now lived on Long Island. They spoke every week. Their parents had both died when Jonathan and Emily were in their early thirties. Before either of them had children. They'd died three years apart, different forms of cancer. Jonathan often thought of how good his mother would have been with Theo. Emily, herself, had an innate talent for being with

Theo, able to talk to him and love him at every stage. Jonathan had grown up nurtured by Emily's and their mom's maternal love. Carly had once said that a man with a close sister made a good husband. He wondered if this was true. Not good enough, apparently.

An hour later, as Jonathan approached the Jetson at exactly 9:00, he saw Sara Danner on the sidewalk in front of the building, again on her cell phone. Jonathan slowed his pace, hoping she'd be off the phone by the time he reached her. She wasn't, but when she saw him, she abruptly told her caller she'd arrived at work and hung up.

This time, on the ground, neither of them wore jumpsuits, no white safety harness straps tucked between their legs, and no hard hats. Jonathan was freshly showered, in a gray button-up shirt, belted jeans and his ever-present Red Wing steal-toe boots.

He stepped closer. "It's typically bad news to have a DOE engineer keep showing up unannounced. But I don't seem to feel that way about you."

"Oh, I can be bad news, but not for you today. The specs look promising. I'm ready to submit a recommendation for 20,000-kilowatt capacity in solar, panels and rails. We could add carbines too, but that's another conversation."

Jonathan's mind worked in such a way that all other thoughts were entirely pushed aside by building calculations and assessment. Twenty thousand kilowatts didn't add up to him. Doing some mental calculations of the square footage, Jonathan couldn't figure out her methodology.

"Mind if I ask you how you got to 20,000?"

Sara began flipping through her papers. I'll have to find the calculation again, but it was useable roof space, by square footage, times .395 kilowatts per square foot. Simple math, but I could be off slightly based on what the useable roof space actually turns out to be."

"I'll be honest, I imagine this building a thousand times each day, and I haven't really pictured solar panels on it. And I'm unfamiliar with the specs and variables on how many you can fit. But I'm starting to push my imagination."

"I wouldn't mind including in my data packet that the DOB has agreed." Sara held back one side of her hair with her hand, to keep it from blowing into her face.

"Agreed might be too strong as of yet. How about, 'I've been consulted on-site', or 'Mr. Brooks will consider any proposal,' or 'In conjunction with Mr. Brooks of the Department of Buildings, preliminary investigation has been conducted.' Jonathan blushed. This was his flirtatious self. "I've mastered the passive voice after seven years in government."

Sara smiled deeply. Jonathan couldn't help but notice that he liked her smile.

"I'll make use of one of those suggestions." She looked at her watch. "I should let you get to work. But if you have the time, I can show you my full report for your 'consult, conjunction and consideration.' Are you free for coffee or lunch tomorrow?"

Jonathan's heart rate accelerated as though he were still running. Despite his sudden onset of nerves he found himself saying. "How about lunch at 1:30 at Irving Place Café, on 17th Street? All jokes aside, I would have to go to bat for the solar with my office and the developer, and that's a significant ask. I like the idea, but I need to review the specs and see what's in your report."

"Of course! I'll write up my summary and bring it tomorrow."

—

Before meeting Sara Danner for lunch near Union Square, Jonathan ducked into The Strand Bookstore to purchase new books for Theo. He took the steps two-at-a-time to the second-floor children's area. He was determined to find "just-right" books that Theo might read the words aloud to him. He had already decided that he wouldn't ask a bookseller for help, because he couldn't state the reading age of his son. Saying seven would lead him to the wrong books completely.

He picked up a Dr. Seuss and began reading of fictional creatures that hid in showers and closets, jogg-oons, sneedles, and wockets hiding in pockets. He put it back. He didn't want Theo reading made-up words. He wanted basic words that he knew, and that he could also read. Green Eggs and Ham was a possibility though, with short real words that rhymed and told a funny story. He tucked it under his arm and kept searching.

While he moved through the store, a wave of shame swept over him. When was the last time he bought Theo books? When had he stopped reading books at bedtime? They played, and sometimes Theo played and Jonathan did his own reading until it was time for bath, and teeth, and pajamas and bed. He felt sick to his stomach for having taken reading out of Theo's life. There'd been a time that they read two books before bed. He'd stopped when Carly moved out, he realized.

—

When Theo was four, he had his first comprehensive assessment with Dr. Wyatt. He was evaluated over multiple days; cognitive, physical, speech, social-emotional development. Carly and Jonathan both took two days off work and lingered around the hospital together, while the professionals worked hour after hour with Theo.

Jonathan and Carly were by then totally familiar with Dr. Wyatt's office. The artwork, the objects on her desk, the Japanese sand garden on their side of the desk for parents to touch. All familiar and comforting.

But this was the first time Dr. Wyatt eviscerated them.

"Theo is a case where the encephalitis is permanent. He can keep progressing, but these effects are now almost three-years-old. His life is now three-quarters post virus. The encephalitis has done permanent damage."

Jonathan imagined that Dr. Wyatt was actually upset with herself. Had she failed to be straight with them earlier? Was this assessment a year later than it needed to be? He swung between fight and flight as he watched and listened to their trusted doctor. He played back the ER doctors saying it could take six weeks to resolve. He had even gaged way back then that if it could take the average child up to six weeks to resolve encephalitis, for Theo it would take three or four.

Two years ago, Dr. Wyatt had said Theo needed more time. They should have known a year later that the virus had caused permanent damage. They did know, Jonathan decided with a twist in his gut. This assessment was arbitrary, as though it was the first time their calendars synced with Dr. Wyatt's, for her to tell them the truth. The known truth.

Carly came out of the bathroom the night of the assessment and visit with Dr. Wyatt, wearing only her underwear, her hands were on her cheeks, crying. Jonathan will always remember an unfortunate detail about this moment. That he simultaneously admired and criticized his wife's breasts in his mind in the exact moment she told him she was leaving him. Her arms bent at the elbow, to hide her face, as though it were the naked element. Jonathan observed her rib cage that pressed against the other side of her lily-white skin. Her breasts were small and perky, but deflated from two years of nursing Theo. Yet Jonathan could identify how they felt in his hands, wonderfully soft and a little bit empty.

"I'm sorry. I barely have the strength to utter these words, but I can't keep going. I can't do this like you. It's not working." She'd covered her breasts then.

The moment Jonathan had anticipated for two years and ten months had arrived. And maybe he had just been strong enough to outlast Carly. Part of how he kept going was the satisfaction that he wasn't doing what he knew she eventually would. The fact that he had what sounded, even to him, like a ready response, tipped him off that he had been waiting.

"You can decide to walk out on your husband. But that sounds like you're leaving your son."

"Oh, Jonathan, Damn it! We'll do this fifty-fifty. And I've been doing it a lot more than that!" And then finally, the sadness behind the anger. "It's not like we help each other, emotionally."

She curled on to the floor. Jonathan observed the notches of his wife's fine-boned spine poking through the alabaster shell of her back. He watched the way her ribcage expanded and fell with each ragged breath. And then as if she were Theo, and the many times he'd soothed his mysterious emotional pain, he sat on the floor and stroked Carly's back.

When her sobbing subsided, she whispered, "Thank you, Jonathan."

—

Jonathan had enjoyed, all to himself, the discovery of Theo reading for one night and one morning. He would tell Carly that night or tomorrow at the latest. He was starting to feel excited to share his happiness with her.

Jonathan arrived exactly on time at Irving Place Cafe. He scanned the small tables for Sara, and then slid into the tight space between a round table and the wall. This may not have been a good place to meet: crowded, noisy and no table service. Somehow the thought of waiting in line at the counter to order embarrassed him. He would pay for both their lunches; he'd invited her. But would she be the type to object? Would she be the type to never reach for her wallet even if they went to twenty meals together? He was regretting the invitation— already resenting the additional complication in his life. Then he scolded his hyper-active imagination. A sandwich. That's what's happening here. Nothing to do with impacting Theo, with sleepovers, with learning about one's personal history or family. A sandwich.

Jonathan pulled his reading glasses from his breast pocket and pulled out the weekly schedule of construction for the Jetson, making quick adjustments with a red fine-point pen. Work grounded him.

Suddenly Sara dropped onto the seat across from him.

"It occurred to me it was presumptuous to appear at the site yesterday, and to assume you'd share my enthusiasm for the solar augmentation. I apologize. I'd like to present my proposal to you."

Her tone was different. Jonathan didn't know Sara Danner well enough to decipher if her seriousness was in itself playful. He remained silent, uncharacteristically tongue-tied.

Sara pulled from her bag three file folders in three colors and began walking him through the various forms, photos, and data packages of her proposal. The papers he looked at were immediately familiar, similar to the paperwork he processed nearly every day for the Department of Buildings. State offices had little variance. She wore a bracelet on her right wrist that was a metal wire which wrapped twice around, there were two very delicate curving tubes of metal strung on the wire. It was the sort of jewelry he bought for Carly when they were married, jewelry which showed its mechanics. Sara was an engineer, like him. Jonathan had sometimes wondered what it would be like if Carly were an engineer or architect. He knew quite a few couples who were both architects. Being in a relationship with someone in his field had always appealed to him. Carly was not that committed to her teaching or her art, and that bothered him.

Jonathan thought now that he should give higher priority to career as a criteria for women he would date. But post-separation, at age 41, he knew that the composite one created for a partner was often based on the hindsight shortcomings of the last partner. Still, he doubted he would date, let alone marry another woman who didn't work. These ponderings were hypothetical because Jonathan didn't date.

For the second time that day Jonathan felt ashamed–this time of his thoughts. He was embarrassed, even just to himself, for turning Sara into a hypothetical love interest, instead of listening to her expertise in green buildings and city planning. It was rude and it was even sexist. He re-focused and played catch-up to hear her proposal, real work she had prepared for this meeting. But quickly she interrupted herself.

"Did you order yet?"

"Oh." Jonathan shook his head. "Sorry. I meant to tell you when you arrived, that we order at the counter." But Sara was already reading the board over the counter.

"I'm going to get a turkey and cheddar on country white. And a hibiscus iced-tea." She reached for her wallet.

"Please let me get it." Jonathan stood. "And I'm going to copy your order too."

They broke from their work briefly to eat their sandwiches.

"I was in a lunch spot like this upstate a few weeks ago." Sara took a dainty bite of her sandwich and wiped her mouth with her napkin. "In Claverack, on a site visit, one of those small town groceries and sandwiches places. I asked for a sandwich, and the owner told me she wasn't making sandwiches that day, since her staff were out. But the funny thing is, the woman was standing behind the counter, eating a sandwich, and there were no other customers in the store." Sara made a go-figure face, that changed her appearance totally.

Jonathan laughed genuinely. "That's the sort of interaction I might have, and not realize how peculiar it was. I would just think, ah yes, she's busy eating, and there's no one here to help."

Sara nodded while chewing. "Me too, but presumably the owner of a small town sandwich shop wants to sell sandwiches."

Jonathan watched Sara pick up from her plate a fallen piece of cheese with her fingers. She returned his gaze while she chewed. Jonathan's spirits had lifted and he was tempted to take out the children's books he'd just bought for Theo and explain to Sara the recent heady development. But, no. That wasn't right. Theo's inner circle got this news. Not Sara Danner, no matter how perfectly lovely a person she seemed to be. Besides, he assumed that Sara hadn't pegged him as a father, and what business of hers was Theo's existence at all, let alone that he was just discovered able to read?

Once they got back to their discussion of the Jetson, Jonathan willfully focusing on the documents, he could easily agree to Sara naming him in her proposal. Sara's report to her own office would not include anything written by Jonathan, from a partner state office. But she would include that they had met on site, discussed the feasibility and that he–the DOB representative–was in support and would forward the proposal to the developer.

They both returned their papers, phones, glasses, etc. to their briefcases and prepared to leave. Jonathan suddenly felt bereft that he would probably never share a meal with her again. How does one go on from one connection to another connection? He couldn't remember how friendships were made—had he ever known?

"Would you like to have dinner with me this Friday?" Jonathan asked.

Sara continued to load her briefcase with the papers she'd spread on the table. She didn't make eye contact with Jonathan this time, but she smiled. Finally, she snapped shut the latches of her bag and looked up.

"I would like to have dinner with you this Friday." Sara blushed slightly. Together they sounded like a Dr. Seuss book, Jonathan thought with pleasure.

Jonathan walked briskly back to the Jetson. Unadulterated pleasure bloomed in his chest. He felt an endorphin rush start near his aorta and his heartrate rose to double pace. He laughed a little at himself too, because he was proud of this accomplishment—a date.

6.

CARLY CALLED Aimee on a Sunday night to make a change to the regular schedule.

Aimee had put Carly's number in her phone when she began working with the Brooks, but she was certain this was the first time Carly's name had popped up on her phone's screen.

Carly rushed right in to explain. "I think Jonathan told you we need to change our Monday morning routine for Theo's physical therapy assessment tomorrow. He's going to miss school."

"Yes. Mr. Brooks already asked me. I'm free to work the whole day. He said Theo might sleep at your house and I said I could come there."

"Oh great. Thank you, Aimee! Please use our first names, call me Carly." Carly laughed nervously. "You're so responsible; I wasn't as organized when I was your age. I'm still not! So, I just found out that an important meeting came up for me at 9 a.m. His assessment is at 11:00. Could you come watch him at my place and I'll get home by 10:30 and we can take him to physical therapy together?"

"Sure." Aimee jotted down the address on Clinton Street in Fort Greene, now curious to see Theo's other home, where he spent most of his weekends with his mother.

Carly wore a vintage black blazer over a ruffled collar, slacks and black two-inch heels. She'd applied lipstick and mascara too, Aimee noted, something that neither Carly or Aimee did on a daily basis. Aimee thought Carly looked great. They were both small-boned and probably wore the same size clothes, but Carly was a few inches taller than Aimee. She looked like she was of Irish descent, she and Jonathan both were, Aimee had been told by Jonathan. Carly was a type that Aimee admired at home, fair with blue eyes, and very dark and very straight hair. A Galway girl. Not a freckle-face like Aimee was. Looking at Carly's put-together appearance, Aimee pushed her own hair behind her ears, where it's unruly mass would stay put for a time.

"Thanks so much for shifting our plans. I'll get home in time for us to take the train together. Help yourself to anything to eat."

"It's all grand. Hi, Theo." Theo had scooted up behind Carly in the hallway. He was fully dressed and with more care than Jonathan usually applied, who always seemed to find T-shirts and sweats in Theo's dresser drawers. Today, Theo was wearing denim joggers and a flannel shirt. Carly lifted Theo. He wrapped his arms around his mother's neck and they kissed each other.

"Wish Mama luck. I'll be back soon."

"Back soon," Theo parroted.

Carly let Theo slide back to the floor. Then she reached out to Aimee for an awkward hug, awkward because it was spontaneous, and they'd never hugged before.

"Bye." Aimee said as they separated. She withheld her, *good luck,* since Carly hadn't said what she was doing.

After locking the front door behind Carly, Aimee was surprised to realize she didn't know Theo's whereabouts in the unfamiliar apartment. She turned into the living room. The apartment differed from Theo's other home. It looked more like a Dublin flat to Aimee. Less natural light made its way through the windows than the top-floor apartment where Jonathan and Theo lived in Carroll Gardens. What struck Aimee the most was the global appearance of Ikea furnishings. Her own studio apartment in Prospect-Lefferts was furnished from Ikea, what little furniture it had. In this realm, international students and divorced moms walked the same territory: clean, new, cheap furnishings, purchased all at a go. Jonathan's brownstone apartment by comparison was full of sunlight and contained what she'd learned from him was 'mid-century' furniture. Carly had started over and didn't seem to have any of the things they might have owned together. Why had she left with nothing?

On the far side of the living room, a white wrought-iron child's bed was tucked against the wall. A quarter of the living room had been artfully arranged to make a wall-less bedroom for Theo, and on the floor beside his bed, Theo sat, laughing at finally being discovered.

"Found you!" Theo shrieked.

"No, I found *you*." Aimee replied. She sat on the iron bed, with its white coverlet and she lightly bounced. Beneath her fingertips, the cotton eyelet pattern reminded Aimee of her own childhood bed, and of how her mother had added lace trim to her nightgown hems and pockets. Pauline had been overjoyed to finally have a girl; Aimee's father had told her many times. Aimee could recall the smell of her mother's laundry too, the detergent, and the sharp clean scent of bleach. But even a girl hadn't been enough to keep her mother alive.

"Show me your things, Theo."

Theo picked up and raised overhead a flashcard with a "B" on one side, and a baseball illustration on the other.

"A-B-C flashcards. Do you know what letter that one is?"

"B."

"Brilliant." Had Carly just shown Theo that one before she'd arrived? Aimee kneeled on the rug and stirred the pile of flash-cards on the floor like a Tarot reader. "Pick a card, any card, step right up and try your luck." Abruptly she stopped her hand. "Ta da!"

Theo laughed.

Aimee raised the letter "T." On the back was a funnel-like illustration of a tornado. *Are they serious?* A tornado was hardly a recognizable symbol to a child, how about a tiger, a turtle?

"What letter is this Theo?"

"T."

"Well, whad'ya know? Your mum is teaching you letters, I see." Aimee was gratified by this. What obsessed Aimee was Theo's physical development. He was seven and crawled to get where he wanted it to go. What Jonathan and Carly called scooting. Aimee's studies on human development and neurology, her life-experience of growing up on a farm, and the research she had been doing to further help Theo, all led her to believe that he had the ability to control his major muscles but hadn't found it. Aimee thought of Theo clinging to Carly that morning, kissing her goodbye. Every night when Jonathan came home, Theo clamped himself onto his hip like a koala bear cub. To prove it to herself, Aimee stood and beckoned Theo with her arms.

"Come here, Theo-mio, let's go to the kitchen."

Theo scooted over to Aimee. Aimee hoisted him up and Theo's thighs squeezed her waist. As a rule, she never lifted Theo, and he seemed to know something was up too.

"Theo, hold me tighter with your legs. Really, really tight." Theo did as he was told. Aimee was equally frustrated and vindicated.

Aimee lowered Theo to the floor. "Come on."

Aimee didn't know why Theo was at Carly's on weekends, and lived with Jonathan for the five weeknights, especially since Jonathan worked full-time and Carly did not. Aimee was overly forthright by nature, and might well have asked, but this arrangement was too unexpected for even her to ask. Obviously, there would be some explanation why a mother would have less contact with her child. Given her own mother, Aimee wondered if alcohol or drugs were an issue.

Aimee had been told that Theo's disabilities stemmed from an illness when he was one-and-a-half. Encephalitis. A virus that affects every person differently. As does most everything. Theo seemed to be an individual who had permanent damage to his brain from the injury of the virus. Aimee just didn't buy that. Every day he grew and learned something. Any day his brain might just right itself and say enough of that setback.

Though in Aimee's life, she had never seen damage undone.

She recalled one heifer of theirs in Ireland. She had birthed every other year, three healthy calves in a row and then the fourth came out with legs that wouldn't hold it upright, the shakes, and murky blue blind eyes. Same organic grain and grass, same clean boarding conditions, same pre-natal care, but this fourth-born was a neurological wreck. Aimee's father shot the calf in the head. Sometimes there just was no reason.

When it came to Theo, Aimee rejected the idea that he was stuck with permanent outcomes. It was five and a half years after his illness. She'd read that adults with encephalitis might take years to recover. One day at a time, as they say. She only saw that there were things to be done.

She was twenty-three years old, three thousand miles from home, caring for the little boy of virtual strangers, and boiling over with anger about the lost time. *Did they need me to come from Ireland to rescue their only child?*

Aimee stopped in front of the closed door of Carly's bedroom. A faint odor came through the door. Aimee knew the smell of turpentine. She hesitated and then opened the door a crack, just wide enough to find out why a bedroom would smell like a workshop. And to be honest, to learn more about Carly herself.

On an easel in front of the window, stood a painting of Theo, sitting outside on a bench with a balloon tied to his wrist. His hair was the blond overgrown mop that Aimee had grown to love as intrinsically part of Theo, and the balloon was a startling red. The painting looked like a photograph, but with texture and depth. It was hard to look away. She saw other paintings around the room, leaning against the walls. Aimee longed to walk in and study them, take them in. But she felt like she was looking in Carly's knickers drawer. She knew she was snooping. She backed out and shut the door again.

On the kitchen table, Aimee found an arrangement of ingredients and a note from Carly. *You guys can make corn muffins if it sounds like fun.*

Theo climbed into his Stokke chair, the exact chair he had at his father's. Aimee felt him watching her read the recipe on the cornmeal box.

"You want to bake?"

"I want to eat."

"You're nobody's fool, Theo Brooks."

Theo dumped the corn meal, the salt, the sugar, the milk into the bowl. He mixed the batter for five long minutes, as Aimee urged, "more," whenever he stopped. Aimee watched Theo's small bicep move under the skin.

"You're going to have to get a lot stronger, me lad."

Theo laughed.

Aimee and Theo were eating muffins with raspberry jam when Carly returned home.

"Mmm, you made the muffins." Carly washed her hands at the kitchen sink and sat at the third chair at the table. She lifted her chin up toward the ceiling and sighed with satisfaction.

Carly ate a muffin in several bites. "Delicious. Can I show you something?" Carly stood.

Aimee looked at Theo in his raised chair, the buckled straps around his waist and chest, making it appear like Theo was wearing a backpack while sitting in a kitchen chair, but this way, he didn't slide down.

"Finish your muffin. We'll be right back." Carly said.

Carly glanced back at Aimee shyly before opening her bedroom door, making Aimee blush with shame for having let herself in an hour earlier.

When the door was swung open wide, Aimee saw that the room contained many finished canvases. The frames were large, anywhere from two to five feet, squares and rectangles, and they were all depictions of Theo. Carly clearly favored red and purple, but the portraits were saturated with every color, rich blocks of cornmeal yellow, amber, crimson, fiery orange, a nighttime blue, and the subject with his long disheveled hair— more blond in the pictures that depicted a much younger Theo.

In every picture he was engaged in some activity, pushing a toy, eating a strawberry, his face buried in flowers, reaching for a dog from his stroller, reaching his arms up to be lifted, sleeping across his mother's large bed, which sat in the center of these portraits.

The room had one window, with an easel and wooden chair beside it, the painting of Theo with a red balloon, propped within the easel. Carly's bed took up the center of the room, and the paintings propped in a complete ring around the walls, facing inward, almost on display. It reminded Aimee of the art studio in Dublin where she'd posed nude for money one semester. And strangely it also reminded her of a time she went snorkeling in Thailand with some college friends and got caught in a school of Snapper fish, a funnel that churned all around her darkly, jaws hinging, magical and frightening.

So here Carly went without her actual son and spent all her time creating him.

"I just came from a gallery. I'm going to have a show. Of these."

Aimee nodded, but never took her eyes off the paintings. She was studying the Theo revealed there.

"You're the first person besides the gallery people and Theo to see these."

Aimee tried not to gawk, but she just wanted to look at them until something they were trying to say became clear. It was like being shown a pile of evidence, but no way to know what crime it solved.

"Well, we should get going to therapy."

Aimee trailed Carly back to the kitchen. She wanted to comment on the paintings, to praise them, but wasn't sure how. They were realistic in a way that photos would be. She knew every moment was real as a captured moment. But why didn't she trust or believe the images?

—

Sitting in folding chairs on the side of the room while the therapist worked with Theo, Carly and Aimee behaved as they did each week despite the fact that Aimee had just been in Carly's home for the first time and had seen Carly's paintings. Aimee kept thinking about the child in those paintings. It was easy to imagine she didn't know that child and then what did she know of the real Theo? She grew agitated at what felt like a puzzle—an unpleasant riddle.

"Jonathan told me you got Theo a staircase." Carly interrupted her thoughts.

"Yes. He practiced on the stoop with me one day, but Mr. Brooks—Jonathan didn't like that." Aimee heard the holy joe tone in her own voice.

Carly nodded knowingly. "Jonathan didn't seem to know that Theo has climbed stairs. I tell him what he does in all his therapies, but he doesn't always hear."

The therapist lined up six cards on the table in front of Theo. From where they were sitting, the women could see some were solid colors and some had pictures.

"Which one is the beach, Theo?" the therapist asked.

Theo immediately touched the card that showed yellow sand, blue water, a striped beach umbrella.

"Good. And blue, which card is all blue?"

Theo touched the blue card as well.

"Very good. Beach and blue both start with the letter 'B'. Can you show me the letter "B'?

There were three letter cards on the table. Theo touched the letter 'D,' but then moved his fingertips to the 'B.'

"Very good. That is 'B.'"

Theo laughed and glanced at Carly and Aimee.

"Did you tell him Theo's learned his letters?" Aimee asked.

"He's only just begun."

Aimee looked away and watched Theo. She thought again about those muscles twitching as he stirred the muffin batter, and of his strong legs, able to grip on command. These were gross motor skills and muscle control that weren't being taken advantage of.

"I'm thinking about the way he gets around."

"How so?" Carly asked.

"I'm studying child development. And I'm using what I know with Theo. He can do a lot more physically."

"I had to teach him to crawl. After he had already walked, but then lost the ability. You know Theo's history, right?"

Theo was now matching like cards with the therapist. Two gold fish, two ladybugs, two sailboats, two stars.

"I know he had encephalitis at around fourteen months." Aimee briefly imagined herself as a young mother, as Theo's mother, and how diligently she'd do all the therapies, the unde-featable team she and her son would make. "I just think he can move about the world in a more appropriate way."

Carly sighed with a weariness that Aimee wasn't feeling at all. Weary was not part of Aimee's repertoire.

"Theo's in therapy four times a week, two of them with quali-fied physical therapists. I'm here at every therapy."

Carly's face looked cross. Aimee knew she was offending Carly, being pushy. But she wasn't quite done speaking her mind.

"Mrs. Brooks—your paintings are beautiful. I love them. But why is it that in all those paintings, I can't tell that Theo is physically disabled? In any of them." Aimee didn't sense it coming, but she was suddenly in tears. She swiped at her eyes, horrified. "There's no painting of Theo scooting on the floor or being carried in public."

Carly opened her mouth to speak and then shut it again. Both women watched while Theo matched two cats, two moons, two teapots, two ponies.

"I paint Theo exactly as I see him. They're all actual moments. That's how he looks." Carly's words trailed off.

"Sorry," Aimee said, in a way that didn't take it back.

Carly had an open moleskin journal on her lap, as always, where she jotted down questions and feedback for the therapists, while she watched therapy. Aimee watched as Carly drew something with her pen, scribbled herself a note.

"You think it's time for Theo to get around differently?"

"Yes, I do. And I think it's my job to say so." Aimee looked straight ahead.

"You've seen him use a wheelchair here. He hasn't shown the spatial reasoning to maneuver one on the streets. It wouldn't be practical in the apartment."

"He tries it once a month for thirty minutes. Have you ever learned a skill at that rate?"

Carly stared at Aimee, considering her words. "I should ask for more time with the wheelchair, you're saying."

Aimee looked at Carly, nervously and defiantly at once. "You and Jonathan are the experts when it comes to Theo. No one else knows him like you do."

Carly shuddered at how Aimee's words echoed Jonathan's from those long years ago, when Theo first became sick.

Theo

MEE-MEE come to Mommy's house. She stir A-B-C cards on floor. I yell them out and she look so surprised. We laugh because I know them all.

Mee-Mee goes in Mommy's room and sees the paintings. I think Mee-Mee likes them.

Mee-Mee need a friend, and Mommy need a friend too.

I stir the batter like Mee-Mee stir cards. Round, round, round, make letter O over and over. I say in my head O, over, O, over and over, on and on. My arm starts to burn, but Mee-Mee say, More!

7.

JONATHAN WIPED tears from his eyes with his knuckle. His face was flush with the drink. He couldn't remember the last time he had laughed so hard. They were as obviously giddy as two people could be on a first date in a quiet restaurant. Sara tapped her fingers on the table top, studying him and looking pleased to have made him laugh.

"I'm serious," Jonathan moaned. "Please stop. I've looked into it. The Jetson could easily install over a thousand commercial composting toilets." He exhaled another laugh and reached for his Old-fashioned.

"Is that approved by Browncage? Maybe he should start his own line of toilets."

"Did you just make a poop joke?" Jonathan asked with approval.

Sara said, "Poop? Who says poop?"

"Oh. I guess kids do." His brain fired sets of chemicals that had been absent all evening. *Have I done anything wrong? Did I hide this information too long?* And lastly, a physical sensation of simple accomplishment, *I am a father.* "And dads. I have a seven-year-old son."

Sara responded carefully. "You're divorced?"

"Separated. Three years."

The waiter brought a long-stemmed glass of red wine and a curved pint glass of beer.

Jonathan took his wallet from his back pocket. He pulled out a school portrait of Theo seated on a hard chair, his hands folded in his lap, his wavy hair nearly touching his shoulders. He was smiling, exhibiting his over-sized front teeth. As Jonathan handed the photo over to Sara, he saw all its details in his mind's eye. He hadn't removed the photo in a long time, but knew it perfectly.

Sara smiled at the picture and Jonathan was flooded with the knowledge that Sara couldn't see that Theo was disabled. *Let it be so, just for right now, just for this night.*

"He's very cute. A young Jim Morrison. Seven, you said?"

"Ha, that's a good one. Yes, he's seven. He's with his mom on the weekends."

Jonathan felt self-conscious informing Sara that he had the weekend free, and he was also exhilarated. The potential of a romantic weekend felt like the purpose of being alive. Even though for three years, he hadn't made such use of a weekend.

"What's his name?" Sara handed back the picture.

He almost said "Carly."

"Theo. I'm sorry I didn't mention him earlier. It suddenly feels like maybe I should have."

"It's our very first date. There are no rules to disclosing your parent status. And if there were, I suspect that even the second date would be early enough. I, for the record, do not have children and have never been married."

Jonathan's face warmed in appreciation. This was his moment to say that Theo had special needs. The words were right there for him, on his lips. But a mixture of emotions and ideas swirled within him. *"It's our very first date."* Did that imply there would be *more? But still, Theo's issues don't need to be trotted out. Sara doesn't need to know my child's capacities. And finally, Theo's disabilities do not lead to feeling sexy.*

The conversation moved on, away from Theo, away from their histories. They finished their drinks, and the restaurant beyond their table was almost forgotten. Until they both noticed that they were the last table.

"What if I asked for the check and we had a nightcap at my place?"

Jonathan hadn't uttered words of that nature in twelve years. Since Carly left, his apartment had been a fortress for Theo and himself. Whether Theo was home or not, there had not been room for a romantic tryst within those walls. Prior to that it was a family home, a struggling little family of three, and the five years before Theo's arrival, just he and Carly, a young married couple making a home and anticipating a bright future.

As typically happened to him in the past three years, when he found someone attractive, he immediately felt an utter lack of space for it. There just wasn't room in his life, mentally, physically, emotionally. His personal life, his son, his ex-wife, even his childhood, his sister and parents' lives, were off-limits. He would not allow anyone into these spaces, which were so highly managed and balanced by necessity. It was like a swaying stack of blocks that he couldn't trust anyone else to add to, only him.

But something had changed. He was inviting Sara to come home with him and he was desperately hopeful that she would say yes. He wanted to bring a woman, Sara, home.

She was smiling and he had his answer.

He gestured to the waiter for the check. And when he reached back into his wallet for his credit card, under the table, he slid out Theo's photo again and silently thanked him for being his, and for not being home.

When they stepped into Jonathan's apartment, he turned on the light and shut the front door behind Sara and they both turned and stared at the giant blue staircase. Jonathan hadn't remembered its presence. His mind quickly circled the apartment taking inventory of all the evidence. Theo's bathroom contained a bench in the bathtub, a raised armrest around the toilet and a large package of diapers on the floor. He could keep Sara out of that bathroom; there was another one off the master bedroom that was his. The kitchen had toddler utensils and bibs, but a non-parent wouldn't register that. However, this staircase required comment.

"This isn't a Mr. Goodbar moment is it?" Sara half-joked.

"Interesting. Theo's nanny purchased this as a gift. Theo is in physical therapy." He stopped there.

"Nice gift."

"Well I had to pay for it. But she kindly chose it. It says a lot that I'm still very happy with this nanny. Let's get that drink. We can have it in the bleachers," he nodded toward the staircase, "or on the couch."

Jonathan walked toward the kitchen, hoping Sara would follow and that the staircase discussion was over.

They sat on the couch, each with a Lillet and soda, a small orange peel nestled in the glass.

"Cheers." They said at the same time. In his home, in the shadow of the staircase, Jonathan felt magically and disappointingly sober.

Sara had freshened her lipstick, he noticed. He had directed her to the master bathroom, while he'd made their drinks. She wore a tight black t-shirt and black jeans. He'd found the shine on her face attractive in the restaurant, and he found the touched-up make-up attractive now. He noticed her arms while she raised her drink and then replaced it on a coaster on the coffee table. He hadn't seen her bare arms before this evening. They were golden brown and toned. Carly's arms were slim and muscular too. She said from carrying Theo.

"Why is your son in physical therapy? If you don't mind my asking."

Jonathan placed his drink, untouched, onto the table. Sara's arm now stretched straight out, to grip her raised knee, her bare heel resting on the couch's edge. In the same way, he might stroke unfinished wood to feel the grain, he had an urge to glide his fingertips down the length of her arm. He desired this even more because he knew it was imminent.

"I could explain that now." He looked at her lips and then into her eyes. "Or I could kiss you. And get back—"

"Kiss me."

Sara didn't move, which was what Jonathan wanted, and he leaned over her arm, and kissed her mouth, full on, and then the upper lip and then the lower lip separately. The level of pure chemistry she aroused in him, made Jonathan dizzy. He pulled back and smoothed his fingers along the length of her arm, the way he'd foreseen doing a minute earlier. Sara sighed. As they fell into each other, mouths together, shifting their bodies every few minutes, touching new inches of skin: a shoulder, a slice of belly between shirt and pants, a jaw, a neck, the new allowance of touch brought back all of Jonathan's inebriation, but it was a sober heat that filled him with a brilliantly mortal feeling.

Once or twice before Jonathan had experienced instant and mutual attraction that was then fulfilled. With Carly it had not been this way, but rather a third or fourth meeting at a mutual friend's home, where he wondered how he hadn't noticed her sexiness before.

He and Sara were insatiable, energized and singular in their abandon. As rarely occurred for Jonathan, he felt only one way about the situation—into it. And even while they removed all their clothes and explored each other, Jonathan could appreciate the moment they'd met on the roof, and that both their eyes had held the eventuality. Physical attraction had been there for them at first sight, and now it got its day, first on an oversized couch that had never been used thus, and then again with more attentiveness and something more cerebral, yet still fueled by chemistry, in Jonathan's bed, ending with the spooning of two spent bodies overcome by sleep.

—

When Jonathan awoke early the next morning, after registering that Sara Danner was sleeping in his bed, his waking mind needed to establish and re-establish that Theo was not at home. In succession, he dismissed the usual demands: take him to the bathroom, put on underwear, choose breakfast food, on and on. Sara was sleeping beside him and Theo was at Carly's. He breathed in and out slowly, consciously. He looked to the window that had a view of sky, and the top corner of the brownstone across the street. How he would engage with Sara this morning was a total mystery to him. His breathing was too shallow and his head hurt.

Neither Jonathan or Sara could sleep past 7:00 a.m., even on a Saturday, even on the morning after a night of drinking and first-time sex. When Sara opened her eyes, Jonathan watched as she registered her whereabouts, the person beside her and the circumstances all in an instant. She laughed nervously. She didn't reach out to touch him but pulled the thin quilt all the way up to her chin, and looked around the room, at the cherry wood wardrobe, the framed artwork, the walls and window, and low bookshelf opposite the bed. Had she reached out to touch him, first thing, or worse, initiated a kiss or even sex, Jonathan would have panicked. As it was, he observed his room and its contents through her eyes, and he felt almost calm. There was one framed photo of him in the room. He was eating a vanilla ice-cream cone on the boardwalk at Coney Island. Carly had snapped the shot when she was eight months pregnant. It was part of why they both loved the picture. Carly had framed it and placed it there on the bookshelf, but she hadn't taken it with her when she moved. *Does it seem vain to have a framed photo of yourself in your bedroom?*

"Are you okay?"

Jonathan found her asking this unbearably kind. He propped himself on one elbow facing Sara and nodded. He felt like jelly inside, but he was okay.

"Me too. Can I take a shower?"

He nodded again. "I'll make some coffee. Would you eat some breakfast?"

"Yeah."

Then they both stayed put under the quilt, facing each other, but looking at each other's shoulders.

"Well, I'm gonna get out of this bed now and walk to your bathroom while naked. It's going to be a little hard to do, but I've faced harder challenges."

"I will look." Jonathan said.

"Expected." Sara raised the blanket and sat on the side of the bed. She rose and walked briskly away, laughing but not turning back.

—

On Sunday afternoon Carly brought Theo back to Jonathan's apartment. She had a key to her prior home, for letting herself in when he wasn't there, but Carly always rang the bell downstairs. Respecting his privacy, Jonathan realized, but he couldn't help but always feel a shiver of annoyance, suspecting that she found it more convenient than digging the keys from her bag. When he opened the door several minutes later, he saw Carly climbing the last few steps, with Theo riding piggy-back.

Jonathan was greatly affected from his weekend with Sara, from more endorphins and dopamine flowing through him than he'd experienced in years. And he was self-conscious to be standing before his ex-wife, having just had a woman sleep over, having just had a lot of sex with another woman, only the second woman since Carly, in fact.

When she reached the top landing, Carly bent forward a bit and craned around to see Theo. "Here's your Dad. We made it!" She was panting lightly from climbing the steps with their big boy on her back. When she turned forward again she said, "Can I come in a minute? I need to talk to you about something."

Senselessly, Jonathan felt this was an immediate repercussion from his weekend with Sara. His body registered a minor panic. He had to convince himself that Sara was no longer in the apartment, and then wonder what traces of her might be. And his own appearance, energy, even scent must surely show the after-effects of such physiological happenings.

He said merely, "Yes. Come in," and backed up.

Carly carried Theo over to the couch and sat down on the edge of it with him still clinging to her back. "Okay. Time to dismount, cowboy."

Jonathan approached and realizing he hadn't greeted Theo yet, ruffled his hair, and then bent down to kiss him. "Hi, Boomer." *Could he tell?*

He knew there were no physical signs of Sara's visit in the apartment; he had been expecting Carly and Theo at this time. But he still felt exposed, as though he wore physical evidence of his weekend that was plain to see.

Jonathan looked at Carly sitting on the couch. He drew in his lips uncomfortably thinking of himself and Sara embracing each other exactly where she sat. He had made his bed after Sara left, taking pleasure in the wrinkled sheets that he decided not to remove.

Carly looked great. Her very straight, dark hair was a couple inches longer than usual. As always, she had a sheaf of bangs hanging over her forehead and into her light blue eyes. Aimee had called her "black Irish" after she'd first met her.

He thought he knew what Carly wanted to say. That once again, he wasn't being a good listener. That he'd been remiss in keeping up with developments, namely the stairs, and that she'd like him to really hear her, believe her perspective, to work with her. He was ready to agree, before Carly had opened her mouth.

Jonathan sat in an armchair across from his ex-wife and son. Theo lay on his back on the couch and pressed his feet into Carly's waist, pushing and laughing. Carly absently stroked Theo's bare feet and looked around the room.

"I've been painting again."

"Oh. That's great. I was always sorry you stopped."

"You were?"

"Of course. I guess it seemed like there wasn't any time." Jonathan couldn't recall that they ever discussed her stopping. That she ever expressed needing time or having regrets, but a few years out, it seemed unnecessary to him that she'd given it up. Sacrifices did not get questioned in the aftermath of Theo's illness.

"There wasn't. And I guess I lost the urge. It didn't come back to me right away, but I started again, almost two years ago actually."

"I'm glad to hear it, Carly." Jonathan said. They both grew silent a moment. "What's up?"

"Well it's hard to believe it. But I've got a show. In a gallery in Tribeca. They're going to exhibit my paintings. It's kind of a big deal."

"That's great—congratulations!"

Carly began stroking Theo's bare leg down the length of his shin, her eyes on her son, who seemed like he could be falling asleep. For Jonathan, this was an eerie parallel dimension to his stroking Sara's bare arm in the exact planetary coordinates forty-eight hours previously.

Carly's expression was weary suddenly. "I think you should see the paintings before I take them to the gallery." She never took her eyes off Theo.

"Why? Are they of me?" Jonathan laughed but his gut said something was amiss. His defenses were ready.

"No. But they're of him. They're paintings of Theo, over the years."

Images came to Jonathan's mind. Images he didn't summon and couldn't justify. He was imagining black and white photos of child polio victims from the 1930s. Children in caps, wielding two walking sticks, metal and leather leg braces strapped tight. He also imagined the unfocused, wet-lipped stares of institutionalized children, who used to be referred to, unabashedly, as idiots. Jonathan knew his imaginings were off-base, but his blood pressure ratcheted nonetheless.

"Nothing inherently wrong with painting Theo. Unless you're objectifying our son for artistic recognition." Jonathan disliked himself as he said this. His reaction felt tactical—not to miss a potential point in a conflict. And he genuinely worried about Theo being viewed as an object or an issue, and he suspected Carly would not be broaching it if there wasn't something to worry about.

"Dada!"

Theo pulled away from his near slumber abruptly as though he felt the level of tension in the room. No one could say when was the last time he spent ten minutes sitting with both his parents at once.

"It's okay, Theo." Jonathan said.

Carly whispered, angrily, "I made these paintings for me, to help me. And for Theo, that he could have these beautiful depictions of himself one day. If you were a friend, I'd tell you exactly what it's been like to have three years of living on my own again, to come around to accepting who Theo is, to find him again, and myself, through painting him. This gallery show came up totally randomly. I have no interest in trying to make myself known as an artist—trying to get recognition for my paintings. And that's not going to happen anyway. I'm his mother; I painted him. Then this thing came along."

Carly's face was contorted with tension, her expression was more of hatred than of hurt. He totally understood her hatred. But he would never, especially after three years of being a single dad, let go of the feeling that it was his duty to protect Theo from anything that might harm him.

"Then I should come see them and make sure I feel comfortable. We may not be friends but we are co-parents. So if there's going to be an art exhibit, an *exhibit* of Theo we should both agree to it, not just you, because you made the paintings. Especially because you made the paintings. I'd do you the same favor."

"That's why I said come see them." Carly leaned in to kiss Theo, holding his head for a long moment. "Mommy's going now." She stood.

"Congratulations, Carly." Jonathan said without standing up.

"Pff." Carly had no more words for him. She picked her bag up off the floor and walked out.

—

Jonathan was having trouble sleeping. His insomniac brain had two favorite concerns. What was next for Theo? And what in the heck was he doing with Sara Danner?

Since his discovery of Theo's ability to read he'd been struggling with what came next. He was keeping it secret just for the time being, especially while he and Carly were at odds. But soon he would broach it with her and the two of them and Theo's therapists would build on the development. But for now he tested it daily in playful ways, placing easy words printed on recognizable objects in front of him: milk, eggs, his "Mother Hen" book, even the New York Times, written words that Theo shouted out to him proudly.

He was searching for some rite of passage, a new activity that responded to Theo's new skill, something that was spawned of it. He wanted to start doing something new with his boy. And then at two in the morning, unable to sleep, it suddenly seemed obvious. He wanted to show Theo his favorite buildings.

Fraunces Tavern, on 54 Pearl Street, was originally called the Queen's Head Tavern in 1762, when it was operated by Samuel Fraunces, a West-Indian man who was also George Washington's chief steward. And thus, Mr. Fraunces was given the honor of catering the banquet in 1783 where George Washington bid farewell to the British troops and turned his attention to the Presidency of a newborn nation.

Looking up at the three-story brick tavern, Jonathan said, "This place was first built in 1719 as a tavern. And around 1783, guess who stood right here to declare victory and independence from England?"

Theo shouted, "Seventeen!"

"Close. George Washington. They had a party here to celebrate that the British were leaving. And our first President, George Washington, was the guest of honor. He tromped all over this neighborhood actually. Let's eat lunch here today, just like George Washington."

"George washing tin." Theo sing-songed.

"Interesting. I bet he did sometimes. See these numbers right here? It says 1907. That's not really very long ago. After George-Washing-Tin ate lunch here this building was neglected and fell apart. A group of people called the Sons of the Revolution bought it in 1907 and made it a tavern again. There's a lot of history right here on this ground we're standing on."

Theo was leaning far forward in his jogger stroller to read the 1907 marker intensely.

"Eat lunch?"

Theo didn't always speak about their present activity or whereabouts. He was usually more random. "Yeah—big boy—let's do it!"

Theo lowered himself out of his stroller onto the sidewalk directly in front of the four concrete steps leading up to the tavern. He climbed the steps, not on his knees like he'd been doing at home, but bear-walking with his hands and feet. His small butt pointed at his father. When Theo reached the top, he sat and looked out at the street below.

Jonathan shook his head and unwrapped the bike chain from the stroller to lock it up. "Wait right there, Theo." Once he'd joined his son on the landing, he faced a dilemma. He didn't object to Theo crawling around in children's environments: the playground, his school, etc. But he preferred for him not to make an entrance into restaurants, the post office, stores, on the ground. But here he was, poised by the door, waiting for Jonathan to open it, and already out of his stroller.

Jonathan knew the tavern. Once inside, the historic dining room on the first floor spread out before you. And up a broad flight of stairs, or using the elevator, there was the meeting room, now used for historical talks or private parties, the same room where George Washington celebrated the end of the colonies, the start of America.

Jonathan opened the door for Theo. Theo scooted in and stopped expectantly at the hostess podium. A middle-aged concierge in a black suit and ribbon tie of the 18th century appeared.

"Table for two?"

"Yes, indeed." Jonathan replied.

The host bent at the waist toward Theo. "Hello, young man. You're doing mighty fine today, I see." When he straightened, he said to Jonathan, "My granddaughter has cerebral palsy. Would your son like to see the meeting room, upstairs? We have an elevator."

Did he think Theo had cerebral palsy? He correctly ascertained he was disabled and commented on it; that in itself was an unusual experience for Jonathan, and it felt sort of refreshing. There was no point in explaining that Theo's disabilities stemmed from encephalitis, and not cerebral palsy. No matter what you chose to call it, the effects might be permanent, and the individual might continue to progress. Today Jonathan saw how these two things could both be true. But the day Dr.

Wyatt had first said that the effects of encephalitis were permanent, was an unparallel shock to Jonathan and Carly. They had only ever thought that they had to be patient for Theo's full recovery. Jonathan had smashed a porcelain lamp on the floor when they got home from that visit.

"Theo, let's go see the upstairs before we eat lunch. And a visit to the restroom."

Before Jonathan could direct him to the elevator, Theo began his new bear walk up the staircase. Instead of following, Jonathan stared, mesmerized. It was so close to walking. He was so upright.

As though reading his mind, the maître'd said, "Is he walking?"

"This is the closest I've seen." Jonathan looked the man in the eyes, then bounded after Theo.

—

Jonathan rang Carly's buzzer. He did not have a key. He'd arranged to be an hour late to work so that he could go see the paintings. Theo was at school. When Carly buzzed him in, he pushed the door and took the stairs two at a time. His headspace was that of an engineering inspector; he'd see what there was to see, give an honest assessment.

Carly stood back with the door held all the way open. She gestured for him to enter and then shut the door behind him.

The apartment was cozy and inviting. Theo's twin bed, against the wall, was covered by a white handmade quilt. Several stuffed animals were lined up across the pillow. Tall bookcases held Theo's folded clothes, toys and puzzles and books, and then higher up, Carly's books and objects. There were several arrangements of rocks, shells or pieces of driftwood placed in front of the line of books. Jonathan knew well this habit of Carly's. The gathering of natural objects on trips, and then making these miniature altars when she returned home. She could always remember where the pile of stuff came from years later: Cape Cod, Hawaii, Costa Rica, Italy, although they all looked so similar to him.

"The paintings are in my bedroom."

Jonathan followed her.

Carly's bed was made up with a blue quilt. The curtains were pulled aside on the large window, making her bedroom twice as bright as the living room. He noticed the extra-long, cherry wood dresser against one wall. The first piece of furniture they'd bought together, right after they'd married, and the only thing she'd asked to take. His thumb sought the back of his ring finger and worried the naked spot that used to hold his wedding ring. He pictured the plain gold band in a ceramic cup in his dresser drawer.

Carly had arranged the paintings in leaning stacks around the bed. He could flip through the canvases as though they were prints for sale in a museum store.

"They're chronological. This is all of them. I'll only use about half for the show, but I don't know which ones yet. Start here."

She indicated the stack of stretched canvases that leaned against the left-side of the bed, the side she'd slept on when they lived together.

Jonathan squatted in front of the pile. The canvases were all the same size, 24 x 36. In the first one Theo was about six months old. He was lying on a bed in nothing but a diaper, his arms up over his head. His pink tummy protruding, the top of his diaper gaping. He was smiling and there was one bottom tooth, about a quarter-way emerged.

On Theo's six-month-birthday, Carly felt this first tooth emerging. Jonathan could viscerally recall those days, hours, minutes, when changing Theo's small diaper, snapping on a fresh onesie from the laundry, occupied his mind fully.

Jonathan saw images of Theo so familiar and life-like they each brought a flood of memories and revived a much younger Theo again.

At first Jonathan felt like flipping the canvases was akin to those fast-motion little books, where the image shifted incrementally each page, and flipping through created a moving image. But on second thought, the sensation was that of a live and in-motion Theo. It was more eye-opening than that. Freezing his son in moments of time, the way the paintings managed to do, sharpened his vision in regard to Theo. Time and Theo had never stood still, as he often felt they had.

He moved to the next stack without comment. And this batch put his heart in a vise, because the event of Theo's illness occurred between images. The last image depicting Theo before he came down with encephalitis was of him in the bathtub, looking like a seal pup, popped up amidst the bubbles. His wet, shining shoulders were framed by Jonathan's masculine arms, the shirt sleeves rolled up. Theo's eyes smiled at him, the faceless man outside the frame. Jonathan found he loved the painting. The very next one was Theo surrounded by pillows on a hospital bed.

He moved to the next stack. More details, facts, crystalized for him. All the rest of the paintings were on Mommy time. Theo at age four, laying across Mommy's bed, the bed that was inches away from Jonathan now. His arms reaching for the bright light of the window. Along the right edge of the painting, a line of moving boxes was unmistakable. No matter how few belongings Carly took with her, there was inevitably a surprising slew of these cardboard boxes that he vividly recalled before she left their shared home, and he knew her well enough to know how long they would have stuck around, unpacked.

There were paintings of Theo in Carly's apartment, on the street with Carly, in the swimming pool during therapy, a self-portrait of Theo asleep in Carly's arms on a city bus, even in a train conductor Halloween costume Jonathan never saw Theo in. He noticed some of the clothing as items he didn't know as well. The wardrobe that lived at Carly's, items he'd never washed and folded, that he was only now noticing had more style and flair than what he clothed him in. Jonathan made a note to himself to buy Theo more stylish clothes, skinny jeans and printed t-shirts—the clothes he saw seven year olds all over Brooklyn wearing.

In the paintings Theo looked happy, healthy, whole, alert, asleep, spontaneous, posed, content, sorrowful, engaged, fiery, exuberant, listless, and loved. Jonathan saw nothing to object to. In fact, he wished to possess them all himself. It seemed unfair that they were Carly's, solely because she had made them. When he reached the last canvas he longed to start again. But when he stood, only then realizing his knees ached from crouching, he was too emotionally spent to go through Theo's life in paintings a second time. He craved being alone and revisiting the images in his mind. He doubted he would forget a single one.

Jonathan rubbed his face with his palms. He had no claims on Carly anymore. No claims on the beautiful paintings. No rights to see what she worked on, except what she planned to publicly display, and even that was her choice, her desire to be considerate.

"It's very considerate of you to show me the work. I realize you didn't have to. The paintings are gorgeous and evocative. As his dad, I could cherish them."

Jonathan's gaze rested on the window, then the stacked canvases, then the covered easel, just never on Carly's face. She touched his folded arms.

"Thank you. That's what I hoped for. We both cherish *him*."

He looked at Carly. His eyes filled with tears, but he blinked them back and willed them away. "You have my blessing. And now I think I'm exhausted and need to get to work." He tried to laugh at himself.

Carly laughed with him. "You'll recover. Work always rejuvenates you."

At the front door, with his back already turned to her, Carly said, "You could come to the show."

He stopped but didn't look back to face her immediately. "Oh. I hadn't considered that." He turned toward her, "I'll think about it."

8.

"I DON'T have to be anywhere." Aimee volunteered. "If you want help with dinner and bedtime. Your night is setting to be off-kilter for sure."

Jonathan had stayed late at work, to make up for the hour he'd taken in the morning to see Carly's paintings. Dinner wasn't started yet and it was already near Theo's bath and bedtime.

"That would be really helpful. Thanks, Aimee."

Theo pulled at Jonathan's leg, demanding, "Puzzle on rug."

"Play with Theo, I'll make dinner." Aimee said.

Jonathan watched Aimee walk purposefully away, wondering what she was going to be asking for, or what she had already done that required forgiveness. But mostly he felt happy about this unexpected evening of someone else making dinner, and another adult's company.

"Americans always start a new meal, they're very wasteful. We, Irish, will take the leftovers and build the next meal around it."

"You're right. I probably would have made pasta tonight and thrown out the forgotten avocado and leftover beans in a few days." Jonathan looked around the table happily at the taco fixings that Aimee had come up with: fresh jalapeno, diced red onions, chopped tomatoes.

Aimee chewed her taco heartily as she talked. "And then you'd throw away the pasta leftovers in a week."

"There's no such thing as pasta leftovers."

Theo ate a flattened taco, held together with melted cheese and refried beans. He watched them with what looked like amusement.

"Do you miss home?"

"Ireland? No. I'm not sure it's home anymore."

Jonathan raised his eyebrows with surprise. "It's been less than six months since you left. Actually, I think I read once that for Irish who leave, it is an abrupt cutting-off, but for Irish Americans, who never stepped foot there, it haunts forever as the lost home."

"Hmph, that sounds like something an "Irish American" came up with. I guess I'll visit for Christmas. My old man offered me a plane ticket. I miss him and me brothers, not Ireland."

Jonathan doctored up a second taco with fresh jalapeno and habanero sauce.

Aimee looked at Theo. "Wipe your chin with your napkin." She wiped her own mouth. "So can I have time off for Christmas?"

Jonathan laughed. "Asking almost a month in advance! Wow. Yes, you can. I believe you get two weeks paid vacation in this job."

"Grand."

"Did you see his therapy today?" Jonathan asked Aimee.

"Yeah. I was there with Carly." Aimee refilled her glass from the chilled bottle of water and drank it all at once. "Carly and I are talking about stuff."

"Oh, yeah?" Jonathan had to laugh. "What kind of *stuff*? Something I should know?" He wondered if his romantic feelings for

Sara were softening him in general. Thinking of Sara, he felt the rush of his infatuation for her.

"The ways that Theo is progressing with gross motor skills. The stairs and his crawl. He's changing. Carly now agrees."

Jonathan thought of the bear walk Theo did at the restaurant, a whole flight of stairs on his hands and feet. He hadn't reported it to Carly, nor had he discussed with her yet his discovery that Theo was reading. He figured this was because he and Carly had fought about the paintings. Or was he hoarding the discovery? Was he distracted by Sara? No matter the why, Jonathan worried that poor communication with Carly would only hurt Theo in the end, and yet he was letting it happen anyway.

"Does the therapist think he's changing? That he could do more?"

"*Do more?*" Aimee's face screwed up like she'd just bitten a lemon. "That's the whole business of growing up. Kids change day to day—they constantly have to do more."

Jonathan tensed. It would have been easy to lecture Aimee on his life as Theo's father for seven years. Her mere twenty-five hours a week for four months did not entitle her to this self-righteousness.

"Use your fork, Theo, not your fingers." Theo looked up at him, his fingers in his rice, and laughed.

Jonathan held off on responding to Aimee's comment, noting his sensation of raised blood pressure. As he forced himself to take a pause and not respond, Jonathan's mind looked for new angles on this constant tension with Aimee. She was a child practically, full of self-assuredness and self-righteousness.

He watched her eat; she also preferred to eat chopped tomatoes with her fingers. There wasn't a wrinkle on her freckled face. Her reddish hair fell in a messy tangle around her shoulders. He sensed she was preparing for a rebuke but would stand her ground. He felt for the first time, the paternal force he represented here.

Suddenly Jonathan saw Aimee as a midpoint between himself and Theo. First off, in years. She was approximately that, halfway between them in age. But she was also an odd girl, someone's odd daughter. Aimee was a stranger in a strange land. Did this girl fit in in her own family, in her home country?

She wanted the best for Theo, and thought he, Jonathan, was a hindrance. Their dynamic infuriated him at times, but he wanted Aimee to continue wanting everything for Theo. He liked her fight. And if Aimee was rude to him, young and judgmental, it didn't mean she was totally wrong. It was part of the package.

Jonathan wiped his mouth and fingers on his napkin.

"I think perhaps you're the one person I can hear this from right now."

Realizing Carly's show was now a week away, Jonathan said, "Did you know Carly's been painting Theo? She has a show coming."

"She showed me a few paintings. I was at her apartment with Theo when she went to meet with the gallery." Aimee's nose turned up a fraction, with the telling of this insider-knowledge.

Jonathan felt his face grow warm. "Am I the last to know *everything*?"

Aimee shrugged. "There's nothing more to tell."

Jonathan noticed Aimee's self-satisfied expression. If he was the clueless man, then she was the girl with the clues.

—

The weekend before Carly's show Jonathan had a date with Sara. He had recently stopped counting their actual dates and instead was using the phrase, *dating for several months,* in his own head. He'd told only his sister, Emily, that he was seeing someone.

"I might have a new girlfriend."

"Really?—I'm happy to hear it!" Emily's voice often sounded like an enthusiastic twelve-year-old. In this case, Jonathan appreciated it. He noted her exuberance in this news, even though she quickly veiled it. Jonathan knew she viewed him as skittish in this arena. And Emily had only become more maternal and protective since his separation.

Jonathan and Sara had already discussed that they were not spending the night together since she had to be in White Plains at seven in the morning on a job. They were meeting for dinner in the West Village.

Jonathan wanted to invite Sara to meet Theo. It had not seemed to enter Sara's thoughts yet that she should have met Theo already. He intuited that she was on the same page as him here: that meeting his young son could be postponed indefinitely. But he felt for himself, that after nearly four months of dating, he was entertaining thoughts of their future, and his having a child, a child with special needs, was relevant information. *Would Sara be a good stepmom to a special needs child?* He cringed, at what he saw as his boyish fantasizing. Would Sara even be comfortable around Theo? She would be forgiven her ignorance on the subject. But how Jonathan wished she might not be ignorant.

One minute Jonathan thought it was due time for this conversation with Sara and the next he felt miles away from the need for it. He was even capable of thinking, *So what? Theo's disabled. We're all grown-ups here. What's it to you?*

He groaned out loud while he applied some hair product, gazing at himself in the bathroom mirror. Abruptly he flipped off the light switch and went directly to the front door, picking up his wallet and keys.

—

Sara was on the sidewalk in front of the Thai restaurant on West 10th Street, looking at her phone. He observed her from across the street while he waited for the light to change. She was slight and had a dancer's good posture. Her hair was very blond. His favorite feature was her mouth; her upper lip was slightly fuller than the bottom, sometimes making him think of a duck bill. He anticipated that when he reached her, she'd put her arms around his waist and turn her face up for a kiss.

"Hi." He said, standing directly in front of her.

"Hi, Babe." She glanced at him, but then returned her eyes to reading a text. Three seconds later she pressed the phone off and put it in her blazer pocket. "Sorry."

They stood still for a second, in limbo, and then Jonathan tugged her to him, knowing she was on her toes when he held her this way and he kissed her mouth harder than he meant to, turning the kiss into something sexual.

"Hello!" She said afterwards, turning toward the restaurant door.

Halfway through their meal, Jonathan decided to bring up Theo. As he ate his basil sautéed eggplant with chopsticks, he imagined what Sara's reaction might be. He expected a pitying expression and regretful words. There was a range of reactions, he'd found, when telling people that Theo had special needs, but the primary reaction was pity and a sorrowful face.

After Theo got sick, and as time stretched on without him recovering, he and Carly had found their closest friends, especially the parents among them, were the worst—even disappearing altogether. As though Theo's condition might be contagious.

Their non-parent friends were much better. Maybe it just didn't occur to them to do anything other than continue treating Theo like a precious baby.

Eventually time had eliminated the need to tell for Jonathan. People who came into contact with Theo could see for themselves. He didn't tell co-workers or acquaintances; Theo's condition was on a need-to-know basis. No one he worked with on the Jetson knew about Theo, just that he "had a family." Jonathan knew that Carly had her own approach. She had developed a special needs community and gained support and friendship from other special needs parents. Theo had playdates with these kids from school. One outcome of their separation was that Carly became the special needs mom, and he was just 'Dad.' Jonathan felt this arrangement worked for both of them, and being separated, there was no need for unity in who they chose to spend time with.

Only his sister, Emily, got it just right with how to talk to him about his child. And that was in the normal way of every parental inquiry. "How did Theo enjoy Halloween? Did he like the puzzle I sent?" Second to this, Jonathan actually appreciated being asked specific questions about Theo. *Destigmatize the whole fucking thing please.* Emily could also ask direct questions with just the right tone. "Does he understand everything we say? He's moving better!" This was infinitely preferable to having friends or family run away from the situation in silence, as Carly's parents had for a solid year, barely calling at all.

"I need to tell you something."

"Oh." Sara looked up from her plate.

"About Theo. He had encephalitis as a baby. He doesn't walk, and his speech is very delayed."

Sara didn't frown or pout. Her face was unchanged, other than a distant stare. Yet Jonathan imagined her facing an unforeseen dilemma at a work site, a major malfunction that would require whole reworkings of the entire project, a problem that she would tackle by starting immediately. It was not a look of pity or sorrow and Jonathan felt grateful.

"He regressed after the illness, and he was only one and a half. His talking is really quite good, but not so...conversational." He was about to say that he'd just discovered Theo could read. But it occurred to him that Sara wouldn't know what a miracle this was, and what it meant for his future. And besides, he felt with new clarity that he must share this news with Carly immediately. It was her news to have first. His thoughts leapt from Carly to Aimee. She too needed to be told about the reading. His secrecy suddenly felt like juvenile behavior.

"Jonathan, I'm sorry. I know what a devoted dad you are. I'm sure it's not easy." Sara's words came out a little airy, and he briefly wondered if she was thinking of something else.

"So the staircase, you said he was in physical therapy."

"Yes. He's done physical therapy for years. He's in a special needs school and he has physical, occupational, and speech therapy weekly." Jonathan had resolved to keep it minimal with Sara, to not get too in the weeds. He tried to reign it in.

"Needless to say, it takes a lot of me to care for my son."

Now it was Sara's turn to look confused. She wiped her mouth and put her napkin in her lap carefully. "Is our relationship taking too much of you? I mean, are you telling me you need to step back a bit, or a lot?" She laughed shakily. "Because men often have that need about now, even without being single dads."

With both hands he reached across the table and took hold of her forearms.

"No, Sara. I feel like it's time to tell you more about Theo, and about me. I was wondering if you'd come over for dinner next week, so you can meet each other."

Sara stared at him. Did he detect fear in her wide eyes? She blinked and the expression vanished. "Yes. I'd like that."

—

Jonathan stood in the unfinished lobby of the Jetson, staring up and down its length. Something was wrong. He paced it out again, unintentionally counting his steps. Two hundred and ten paces. It took three minutes to walk the main lobby that stretched along 21st Street from Fifth Avenue toward Sixth Avenue. The foundation and subfloor had been laid. The marble slabs had arrived and were due to be installed today, on schedule.

Jonathan paced back to the entrance at Sixth Avenue. There'd be two revolving doors and double automatic swing doors that would operate by pressing a large button outside the building or inside the lobby. There was a bank of six elevators to the left of the entrance that went to floors 1-10. Jonathan stood there, lost in thought. He was an imaginary visitor having just entered from the street, pausing a half second, as he knew people who'd never entered a skyscraper would do, getting their bearings, determining the interiors' facing, north-south-east-west. All felt right, if he needed floors 1-10. He again walked the two hundred plus paces to the western side of the building. Glass ceiling signs which were long-to-come would indicate that elevators for 11-18 and 19-26 were in the back. He reached the back and was seven feet from the empty elevator shafts, toes against a wooden step. He felt stuck, unable to reach the elevators. He stared at the wooden step against his shoe, a nine-inch rise. His hands shook. His jaw tensed.

Jonathan strode back the length of the lobby. Even trying to slow his pace, he arrived in a minute to the raw wood cabinet that held important papers, various keys, and the original blueprints of the Jetson. He unrolled them and rapidly flipped the large thermal pages to the first- floor lobby. Seeing, as he knew he would, that there was no stair at the eastern end of the lobby in the blueprints, made his heart thrum with rage.

Jonathan was the project manager, so this was ultimately his fault; he was responsible for anything and everything. But the "brick and mortar" fact that a step had been added to the lobby was the foreman's mistake. The same foreman who had played with him five months earlier, saying the engineer on the roof, Sara, was a man looking for him.

Jonathan yanked the walkie-talkie off his belt, and paged, "Buckner. Where are you?"

After a pause, the device spoke back to him. "Brooks? I'm on three. You need something?"

"Come meet me in the lobby." Jonathan switched his walkie-talkie off.

He went back to the offending step and waited.

As he approached, Frank Buckner called, "What's up?"

"What is this?" Jonathan's head was down, looking at the blueprints in his hands.

"What is what?"

"This step."

Buckner stared. "Are you sure there's no stair in the plans? There's a gradient here. That has to be dealt with. Does it matter?"

"Of course it matters. Are you trying to tell me that you think you couldn't have laid a single-level floor here accommodating the gradient?" Jonathan put one hand in his pocket, trying to stifle his outrage.

"No. We could have. But we didn't. Your man won't know the difference." This referred to Browncage, who periodically got a walk-thru with Jonathan.

"You know who will know the difference? The person in a wheelchair who has a job in this building on the twentieth floor. There are codes. Surely you're fully aware of wheelchair-accessible building codes in New York City."

"Shit." Buckner shook his head as though a group of gnats were in the air. "Maybe the handicapped can work in the front of the building on 1-10, or we'll build a ramp over there." He pointed to the lobby's southern edge. "That's what we'll do."

"No, that's not what we'll do!" Jonathan was yelling now.

He realized that as he had stood just inside the Sixth Avenue entrance five minutes earlier, trying to sense what was wrong, he had in fact, imagined being Theo. Theo as a grown man, a briefcase laid across his lap, in a fast and efficient motorized wheelchair, entering the building for work, following the sign to the twentieth floor and being stopped short at this step, unable to go further.

"Don't be an asshole, Buckner. Not in my building."

Jonathan roughly rolled the plans in his hands and spun away from the foreman. There was a fix here, a way to rectify the mistake. But Jonathan had no appetite for working it out with his foreman just then. His cell phone rang as he strode away.

"*Carly*" appeared on the phone's face. She never called him during the work day.

"Hi." Jonathan was grateful to be made unavailable to Buckner just then.

"Hey!" Carly was a little breathless. "What are you doing right now? Could you meet me today to check something out together?"

"What, like now? What's going on?"

"I know, its impulsive. But there's something I want to look at together."

"I can't right now, Carly. I'm at work. I'm dealing with a problem." Jonathan took a mindful breath. "Sorry. What is it?"

There was a long pause on Carly's end. "It's okay. I'm just excited. It can totally wait.

Guilt rose from his gut. "Is this about Theo reading?"

"Reading? No...I'll tell you later. It can wait. It's okay. I'll send you a video of Theo in therapy today. He's doing great."

Jonathan was suddenly exhausted. He couldn't be in two places at once. He couldn't even prevent his own foreman from making a huge architectural mistake.

"Wish I could be there with you instead of dealing with my foreman. Can we talk about it tomorrow at the opening?"

"You're coming? You didn't say you were coming."

"I didn't? Am I still invited?"

"Yes, nothing's changed."

"So, you can tell me then. Sorry, Carly. I can't break away right now."

"O-kay," her voice grew bemused in the one word, "So you've noticed he's reading, eh?" There was full-blown teasing in Carly's voice now, and Jonathan knew he wasn't in trouble.

"A few words."

"Ah—a few words—I might have noticed that too. While we worked the letters and phonetics app over and over." Carly laughed. "He's doing great, Jonathan. He's on a roll."

Jonathan inhaled deeply and was filled with gratitude. This was all that mattered.

—

Jonathan filled a plastic cup with wine and turned to the closest painting. He'd glimpsed Carly in the room, she was surrounded by four people, one of them presumably the gallery owner, by his proprietary air. Jonathan would check out the show and greet his ex-wife when she was freed up.

He stood in front of a painting of Theo pushing a wooden train. There were colorful blocks that sat on pegs on top of the train. Jonathan and Carly would be the only people in the room who knew that Theo had easily slid those blocks off and onto pegs at age one, when Carly's parents had sent the train, and then was unable to do it for three years after his illness. Carly and Jonathan had sadly noted over the years that it was nearly impossible for people to give fitting gifts, age-appropriate didn't work in Theo's case anymore.

The painting evoked for him the memory of Theo's body at the time. He had recovered enough by three that he was sitting confidently again, something they took daily satisfaction in. Their boy had re-learned to balance his head on his torso, to sit upright on the floor. And he pushed this train around. That was wonderful too. And he could lift a block with holes drilled in it off of a peg and replace it.

Jonathan remembered a famous poem about a red wagon, that a lot depended on a red wagon in the sun. He understood how a toy train with a removeable block mattered, just like that red wagon.

He wondered, briefly, what the painting could mean to others. It was just an ordinary moment. A pretty child. Who was that painter, Mary Cassat? Maybe Carly's paintings were like that, but sharper, less muted. Mary Cassat meets Edward Hopper. But what did he know? He'd never tell Carly his layman comparisons. He remembered how he'd been impressed by her art school degree. Until he wasn't. Why was it that we stopped being impressed by those we were closest to?

Just then, Carly touched his arm. He turned to her, and they kissed each other on the cheek. In that moment of touching his ex-wife, Jonathan felt his love for her, still existent. He wanted her to enjoy this night. He wished her well.

"Jonathan, you know Patrick." She rested her hand on the arm of the man beside her.

Jonathan extended his hand, "No, I don't believe we've met."

The feelings of three seconds ago showed themselves to be ephemeral. Jonathan felt something messier now. *Who is this muscular man with a mischievous gap-toothed smile?*

"We met at a dinner at Miles Cooper's apartment." Patrick offered.

Patrick had an accent, which Jonathan was working out when Carly completed his thought.

"Patrick recommended Aimee to you. She used to babysit his nieces in Dublin."

"Of course! So sorry, Patrick, nice to see you again." *What was he doing here with Carly though?*

"Aimee has been wonderful with our son." Jonathan gestured feebly to all the paintings around them. "But I'm confused, you weren't at that dinner, Carly, right? How did you two meet?"

Patrick smiled broadly, a wolfish grin.

Carly answered, "Through Miles. About a month ago." She didn't elaborate and the three of them stood there awkwardly.

Jonathan couldn't help but wish that Sara was standing beside him. It was a juvenile desire to level up to Carly having an apparent date. He took a deep breath, despite the fact that his chest felt constricted.

"Well, congratulations, Carly." Again, he waved his hand, with the now empty wine cup in it, gesturing at the walls. "I'm going to make my way around to see them all."

Carly smiled at him, and for a second, Jonathan felt she had forgotten Patrick's presence, and that she seemed to be with him alone. Her smile was sad, he realized.

Half an hour later, Jonathan stood in front of the moving-boxes painting, rendered in the first weeks after Carly left, he guessed. He was remembering what Carly had said after first meeting Aimee. "Do you think Theo will struggle with her accent?"

"How so?"

"It's a bit hard to understand her."

He had an excellent ear for languages and music. Carly was tone deaf and always struggled with accents.

"He'll be fine. Aimee speaks English, and Theo doesn't really speak at all."

Carly had swatted his arm playfully. "I like her."

Carly appeared at Jonathan's side again, on her own this time. "This is so strange. I'm glad you're here; it means a lot to me."

Jonathan had to pull his eyes away from the painting of Theo, wet in the bubble bath, his favorite. "I'm glad I'm here too." He touched her sleeve gently. "You're a really talented painter."

Carly looked distressed to receive this compliment from him; her cheeks blushed, "Thank you."

"So, want to tell me what you called about yesterday? You never sent me the video."

"Oh. Here? Well, why not?" Carly glanced around quickly. She took out her phone and quickly scrolled back a few images and then looked at Jonathan.

"Well, a few weeks ago, Aimee suggested we get more wheelchair time for Theo in therapy. To work on his eye-hand coordination, connecting the joystick with the motion of the chair. The therapist agreed, and we've now had three sessions. Watch." Carly handed Jonathan her phone.

Jonathan instinctually turned his back to the room of people, turned the volume all the way down and hit play. The chair was larger than the last version he'd seen in a video, but still a small, child-size electric wheelchair. Theo only wore one Velcro belt around his hips. He was wearing his favorite NY Yankees t-shirt, and black and white checkered Vans sneakers. But it was his smile that beat the band. He propelled himself forward for about twelve feet. It looked like he was laughing. Jonathan turned up the volume, no longer caring if anyone overheard.

Theo's laugh trilled out from the phone, and as he banked right and leaned his whole torso into the turn he called out, "Vrooom! Beep, beep!" For twenty more seconds, Jonathan watched Theo make purposeful turns around the open therapy room. His newfound freedom of movement lighting up his whole face.

Jonathan watched the video again, sound on from the start.

Carly had called him while he fought with Buckner about the step in the lobby. For many years, there had been coincidences like this between them. It didn't surprise him.

Jonathan had not made this leap to thinking Theo might be ready to utilize a wheelchair. And yet, his mind's eye had no trouble imagining him bringing one home now.

He handed Carly back her phone. "Well, hard to argue with this. 'Vroom!' He's ready to bust a move. Of course, he is." Suddenly it was obvious to Jonathan that his son was busting moves day in and day out. And lately, he was leading the way. Jonathan was trailing behind.

"You think it's time to get one?" Carly asked. "Yesterday, I looked up a supplier after therapy. I called you from the sidewalk, wondering if you'd meet me there right then. I feel so sure of it now. I've watched that video twenty-five times, and I was there."

Jonathan wondered for a second why he himself couldn't have been there. And how different that might be than seeing a video of Theo gaining skills.

"Let's go look this weekend. If he's ready for it, we better be."

Carly hugged him impulsively. "I'm so nervous. Why does happy feel like nervous?"

He imagined Theo guiding his own motorized wheelchair down the sidewalk. They would need to teach him to stop at corners, to be aware of other people, to listen to their instructions, especially stop. But he could see it now.

Jonathan nodded. "The English language needs a new word, happy that makes you nervous." He put one arm around Carly's shoulders. "Buckle up, Carly."

Carly laughed appreciatively.

"Aimee's with Theo, she stayed late. I should go and let her get home."

"Okay." They hugged again and Carly watched him head to the door.

"Oh." He turned and strode back to her. "Are you dating Patrick?"

Her eyes widened. "None of your business. He saved me from coming alone. Handsome guy, don't you think?"

"Very." Jonathan said glumly.

Jonathan stared at Carly. How did these things happen in the universe? You love someone, you have sex with her, you get married, you have a child, then merely move in time, like moving the bar along the bottom of a video, and you're asking her if she's dating someone else.

"Good night. And congratulations, Carly."

—

The electric wheelchair model Jonathan and Carly chose was the EZ Lite Cruiser Deluxe DX12. It was an absolute beauty in Jonathan's opinion, as it should be for $2,595. Weighing 45 pounds and folding down to 10 inches when laid flat, it could easily be popped into the trunk of a car or stowed outside his apartment door.

In the showroom, Jonathan enjoyed listening to the salesman explaining to Theo how it worked. "Push the joystick forward—you go forward, pull the joystick back—you reverse, left—you turn left, right—you turn right; see how sensitive it is to your touch? A light touch is all it takes." Theo moved back and forth along the wide aisle they had for trying out the wheelchairs, akin to walking around a shoe store in new running shoes to see how they felt.

Theo reached the end of the aisle space. He turned the chair to the left and did a 180 to head back. "Excuse me!" He called out softly.

Jonathan turned to Carly. "Where'd he learn that?"

Carly shook her head, laughing. "Are you happy-nervous?"

Jonathan watched as the salesman coached Theo in turning the chair to the right for his next 180. "Try a right turn now. All you right-handed kids, prefer to turn left. You gotta have all your moves down."

"Maybe just happy. Nervously happy."

"And Theo?" They both watched Theo's fixed grin as he controlled the chair and zipped along next to the mirrored wall.

Jonathan knew what she meant. "He's thrilled."

Dr. Wyatt thought the timing of getting the wheelchair was appropriate and would also have cognitive benefits. Theo's brain would have to keep up with his faster mobility. He would negotiate the sidewalk and interior spaces, interacting with his environment and his neighbors with physical give and take, adjusting to not collide. He hadn't used that spatial judgment other than the two months of his life when he could walk and run.

The three of them took an Uber back to Jonathan's with the new chair in the trunk. They went directly upstairs to the apartment, Theo climbing the three flights of stairs, Carly walking up behind him, and Jonathan carrying the folded wheelchair in the rear.

Theo tried out the new wheelchair in the living room. Jonathan moved small furniture and objects out of the way as Theo pivoted around the smaller space. Theo seemed to know in his gut that what he had was a new set of wheels; that what he needed was open road.

"Outside." Theo demanded with a purposeful tone of voice, after trying the wheelchair for ten minutes in the apartment. Jonathan couldn't help but think that the EZ Lite Cruiser was working wonders already.

On the street, they had a dialogue that many New York City parents have with their child who is about to be given scooter or bicycle privileges.

"You must stop before the corner, right here. You cannot turn a corner where we can't see you. If we call stop, you must stop. Don't get too far ahead."

And still they were running behind him as soon as Theo took off at full speed. "Slow it down, Theo!" They both ran behind while Theo shrieked with delight in his independence.

"Don't worry, Carly—the battery only has fifteen miles on it!" Carly stumbled as she laughed and ran.

9.

Aimee's youngest brother, Colin, picked her up at Kerry Airport when she arrived home for the Christmas holiday. She came out to the curb with her one carry-on. Colin was parked in the jeep at the end of a queue of cars. Before she even reached the edge of the curb, he was peeling out from the line to get her.

He scooted out of the front seat to take her bag, not to hug her. "Hey Dodge. You cut your hair."

"Ha!" Aimee touched the uneven ends of her hair, touching her shoulders. "About a year ago. Haven't been called Dodge in a long time either."

"Yeah? What are they calling you in America? Irish Spring? Lassie? Or do they just think you're British?" Colin was pulling away from the curb, holding his arm out the window, signaling. He drove like a safe race car driver, all skills. Aimee suddenly felt the urge to be driving the jeep herself. And she thought of the roads around their farm and the land's bucolic beauty in a way she never had before. She thought, maybe I am becoming American, idealizing green Ireland. Still she looked forward to driving those roads by herself in the days to come.

"They call me Aimee if they speak to me at all. How's Dad?"

"A hundred percent the same. A pain in my arse."

Aimee looked at her brother in profile to see if he meant it. "Why?"

"Shut-up, Dodge. You lose your senses in New York? Your old boyfriend is getting married on New Year's Eve, the new trendy thing to do. Maybe he'll invite you."

"Connor? Jesus, he's marrying young."

"Connor's got four years on you, remember? He's twenty-seven, plenty time to be getting married."

"Are you going to the wedding?" Aimee kept her voice neutral.

"Can't. I'm taking Sheila to a Bitch Falcon concert in Tralee. She loves them. *Shite,* I might propose to her too."

Aimee saw suddenly and brutally how life in Ireland would move on without her. Had moved on already. Her brothers and school friends would marry, have families. They were not frozen in amber as she thought of them. And what would her life be? In New York you were no one. The city didn't notice individuals. She'd sensed that in her first days there and liked it.

But for one New Yorker, Theo, she was someone very important. Aimee saw herself briefly as the sun, and Theo her one devoted planet. She would give planet Theo exactly the right amount of energy, nourishment and gravitational pull to call forth his growth.

Aimee looked out the window. On the motorway, the city retreated quickly into vague industrial yards, semi-trucks parked in twos and threes, huge gravel piles, long aluminum barns, holding the agricultural products, grain or silage, that were always headed somewhere. The ugly in-between land would rapidly give way to real country and their farm in Castlemaine was another hour of driving. She felt like a visitor. It had been a year since her last visit. Five years since she went away to college.

"Who is Connor marrying?" Aimee asked, realizing that of course she would know the girl. Aimee was startled to feel a lump in her throat. The news brought up her deep loneliness. Not just an emotional state for Aimee; she was alone in her life abroad.

"Margaret Farrell." Colin looked at his sister with a taunting smile.

"Margaret Farrell! Well, he never was cruel to her. I remember she liked coming to the deli, always blushing as she said hello to him. I think she counted on his kindness."

"Or she wanted to get in his pants. She went off to college too. But she came back and opened a clothing shop on Main. And get this. She had a breast reduction."

"You're lying!" But Aimee knew he wasn't. It amused her that her brother even knew those words. "Well good for her. She took all that teasing from the age of what, ten, growing double D's before anyone else even had any."

"And she's smart. All I ever saw before was the tits. Maybe you'll buy something from her shop. The clothes are all very hipster."

"Listen to you."

—

Before Aimee and Colin could make their way from the jeep to the house, her father pushed open the back door and strode outside. Aimee saw him from ten paces, the two-story white clapboard behind him and she observed in a new way the man who was her father. He wore a clean long-sleeved flannel tucked into high-waisted jeans, his jean cuffs rolled up, revealing his wellies. He was half-a-head shorter than Jonathan Brooks, but she knew, even fifteen years older, he could out-lift him and knock his lights out.

"Dad." Aimee hugged him around the neck, surprised by her emotion.

Colin strode past them, Aimee's bag gripped in his hand. He would leave it inside her childhood bedroom. The male members of the O'Malley family had always taken gentlemanly care of their baby girl, yet none of them had ever tried to give her guidance in the world, or prevent her from doing physically dangerous farm work or any other risky pursuits. And it had been a natural course of events for her to leave for Dublin and then New York. Unspoken and expected it seemed.

"I figured you'd need lunch when you got here. I picked up sandwiches and soup from Wally's."

"Sounds great." Aimee had been the family cook, starting from age eight, after her mother died. She'd loved finding recipes and cookbooks at the library and making things that were difficult and required special shopping trips. When she left for college, her dad and brothers had taken to prepared foods from the supermarket. Her older brothers all had jobs off the farm and lived on their own. Her dad and Colin now ran the place, with a few helpers every morning to help with milking and other farm chores.

The three of them ate lunch in the kitchen. Aimee told them about school and minding Theo. Her father whistled through his teeth, when Aimee said the child was seven years-old and wasn't walking because of a childhood virus. Aimee nodded while biting into her sandwich.

After lunch, Aimee said she wanted to go to the cowshed and see the cows. Her father shook his head before she could invite him, "I'll clean up this kitchen."

Wearing Colin's wellies and a winter coat and a black ski hat, Aimee slid the shed door open on its runner, feeling the warm bovine air caress her face. Forty cows breathing in and breathing out. It was cold enough outside that all the animals were in the barn, fresh silage piled in their feeder bins, yellow hay loosely spread on the dirt floor to absorb urine and cushion their bony hips. Calliope swung her brown head toward Aimee's outstretched hand, wiped her wet nose back and forth on Aimee's palm, blew wet snot on her. One of the few Jerseys her father had agreed to buy as a calf, because Aimee loved their petite deer-like faces.

"I know you. Do you know me?" Aimee slowly made her way down the aisle, open stalls on both sides of her, two cows per stall, munching on their hay. There were a few identical solid brownies whose names escaped her, perhaps they were born after she'd left. Aimee was afraid she wouldn't notice if anyone was gone without asking her father. But most of them were immediately recognizable. Their black and white or brown and white patterns, their distinctive eyes—light brown to nearly solid black, their stars or diamonds of blank foreheads, their personalities revealed in bared teeth, outstretched tongues, raised lips, ground-pawing, forceful exhales, hide shaking, tail swishing and tap dancing were all familiar and heartwarming to Aimee.

She scratched foreheads and rubbed necks, making her way down the line. Aimee cooed their names, remembering some as calves she'd bottle-fed.

"Patsy, Nanny, Madonna, Nicolette, Jellybean, Shannon, Courtney, Cupid, Rainbow, Sinéad, Eleanor, Queenie," and so on, each name reflecting the animals' age, or rather Aimee's age when the calf was born and named, some her favorite musicians, some her girlish whims.

Aimee walked back up to the house, her hands smelly and moist, her jeans and wellies smeared with muck. Although the milking was automated, she imagined showing Theo the gentle giants and teaching him to milk their rubbery full teats in the early morning, their streams of milk whizzing as they hit tin pails. And then drinking that fresh milk, after chilling it a few hours.

After showering, Aimee gathered her personal items into a small purse, and came downstairs. The jeep keys were dangling on the hook by the front door, but she found Colin seated at a desktop computer tucked in a corner of the living room and asked him if she could use the family vehicle.

"Take it."

"Thanks. See you later." She began to cross the room and then turned back. "Are you online? You have internet here?"

Now Colin took his eyes away from the screen to smirk at his incredulous sister. "We have indoor plumbing too. It's not your fancy Wi-Fi, but we have internet."

Aimee scowled playfully. "I'm not calling you a culchie or anything. It's just I was used to going to the library, that's all."

Aimee sped down their road, leaving two dirt clouds behind her, as she drove to town. Main Street was about five New York blocks long. It had changed though. There was a sleek coffee shop, which did have Wi-Fi advertised in the window, and a new tattoo parlor was a baffling surprise. Did any of her brothers have tattoos now? She'd parked right in front of *Fan and Feather* and knew instinctually it was Margaret's shop.

From the jeep, Aimee saw several young women moving about in the store, pushing hangers, lifting items off the tops of clothes racks. They might very well be some now teenage children she had once minded, or been friends with their older siblings, but nonetheless, Aimee enjoyed a feeling of anonymity. She realized she would be going into Margaret's store, perhaps she was headed there all along. Why not? She'd known her since middle school and Margaret was about to marry Aimee's first boyfriend. Aimee was curious how Margaret would look all grown up. Her thinking was potentially magical. Was Margaret who she might have become? Would seeing her give Aimee a glimpse into a virtual mirror where she'd see herself more clearly?

A bell chimed as she opened the door, and from the register, Margaret looked up and called, "Good afternoon. Let me know if you need some help." She wore a fifties style dress, tight-fitting bodice with a flared skirt, a print of small red and blue dots. A pencil held her red hair high in a sloppy bun. She was more Brooklyn than County Kerry.

Aimee began looking at jeans, wondering what she would say to Margaret. She flipped through an entire rack, and then carried several pairs of jeans to the dressing room to try on. She was experimenting with being twenty-three and back in the hometown she'd left at seventeen. She was not looking for new jeans. When she pulled back the curtain from her small dressing room, Margaret was standing there, jeans folded over her forearm, with fresh red lipstick.

"Did you find anything you like?" Margaret asked.

"Aye."

"We know each other, don't we?"

"I went to St. Anne's. I was a few years behind you. I'm Aimee O'Malley."

"Of course. I know two of your brothers quite well, Colin and Tom."

"Aye, Colin told me about your shop."

"Good of him. Where you living now?"

"New York."

"I'm jealous!"

"You look like you're doing great. You went away to college too?"

"Aye. In London."

"That's grand. I was in Dublin."

"Not too many of us get out."

"And fewer come back." Aimee said, not meaning to make a statement that Margaret had left only to return. She felt sure now that Margaret did know she had dated Connor. "I hear you and Connor Dillon are getting married too. I know him too from St. Anne's."

"More than *know* him. I remember you were always at that deli where he worked. He had eyes for nothing but you back then."

"Childhood sweethearts." Aimee tried to shrink it.

"Around here that's who people usually marry."

Aimee lifted the jeans that were hanging over her bent arm, unsure how friendly their conversation was.

—

On Aimee's second night at home, after dinner, the three O'Malleys sat in the living room with the Christmas tree. Colin and her Dad had begun decorating the tree while Aimee had cooked a roast for dinner. The tinsel was thrown over the front side only, the ornaments placed all at eye level, and the star for the top forgotten. Aimee thought it looked like a nursing home patient dressed by an uncaring aide.

"You two have seen Christmas trees before, right? Even if you've never decorated one." She reached for the base of the tree, which wasn't covered with the red wool skirt her mother had embroidered and pulled the tree away from the wall. "We'll have to strip it down and start over with the lights. Come on, you'll learn how for when I'm not home for Christmas."

They stripped the tree and started over. Aimee alone seemed to know that there were more ornaments, red and gold glass balls, in the dining room hutch. She also knew which closet contained the star, the skirt and the Christmas lights. When it was done, her father appreciatively said, "Now that looks like a Christmas tree."

Christmas morning consisted of Aimee, Colin and their father, exchanging gifts in front of the tree.

Aimee had brought her father a biography of Joe Kennedy as a present. The only thing she'd ever seen her father read was biographies. The Kennedy patriarch had a tragic story. Remarkably he told his children they must go into public service. When Robert Kennedy was assassinated, five years after John, the father was an old man with locked-in syndrome, unable to speak or share his immense grief. He also had a disturbed daughter. He'd elected to get her a lobotomy, which had immeasurably worsened her condition and he'd never forgiven himself for the harm he'd caused his child.

Aimee tried to tell her father all that while he stared at the book cover, the wrapping still around its edges. He raised his eyes toward his daughter, with grief on his face.

"Thank you. I'd like to read this." He said grimly.

"Well, it sounds morose, but it's supposed to be a wonderful read!" She was trying to sell him the gift. She told herself to stop, he would like it or he wouldn't.

Her father gave her a denim purse, studded with rhinestones. It was well-suited for a twelve-year-old.

"It's really cute. Thank you so much." She would give the purse to Theo, maybe put some smaller presents inside it, a few new marbles for his treasured marble collection.

She had brought Colin an I ♥ NY T-shirt. He removed his pajama jacket and put it on, then put his arms back through the pajamas, the farmhouse kept chilly as always in December.

"I'm afraid I didn't get you a gift, Dodge—Aimee. I'll take you for a pint later."

"I'll take it."

—

Aimee's oldest brother, Jack Jr. would be joining them for Christmas. He was thirteen years older than Aimee, and had often seemed more like her father's brother, than hers. He was also the only child already gone from the house when their mum died. He and his wife, Mary, came for the midday meal.

The night before Aimee had pulled a leg of lamb from the freezer in the garage. She'd seasoned it with a dry rub overnight with Mediterranean spices and bay leaves and she was slow cooking it all morning for their Christmas meal.

She looked up from peeling potatoes in the kitchen to see Jack Jr. enter the room. He placed a bottle of wine wrapped in gold foil on the counter before seeing Aimee there, wrapped twice around in an apron.

"Merry Christmas, Mum." He said with a stutter.

Aimee pushed her hair away with her wrist, and opened her palms to the air. "What the heck?"

"Dahn't know why I'd call yer dat!" Jack Jr. awkwardly kissed her cheek. "You're a wee lass. But something made me see her just now."

Aimee tried to laugh it off. He seemed as always, a different generation to her, not of the present times and just vastly older than her and even Colin and Michael. He was an enigma when she was little and still was.

Throughout the afternoon, Aimee noticed how little her family talked. Long silences stretched while they ate, broken by half sentences, utterances that required no response. She began to track how many times a comment responded to the prior one. Her dad and Jack Jr. said almost nothing at all, and she wondered when Jack Jr. had begun to stutter. Had he always?

As she cleared their dinner plates, crossing through the living room, her eyes fell on the computer. She signed in to her email and wrote a short message to Jonathan Brooks.

"Merry Christmas. How's Theo doing? I forgot to tell you, he likes the plain yogurt with a drizzle of maple syrup. I'm writing you from Castlemaine, so I guess it isn't just a job to me." She added a smiley face emoji.

—

Aimee was sleeping in her childhood room. The boys had shared bedrooms, two to a room. Even though she was the last child, from birth she'd been given her own room. It was unchanged from how she'd left it at eighteen when she moved to Dublin.

The day after Christmas, Aimee awoke abruptly, and without thought, swung out of bed and crouched in front of the old wooden dresser and slid open the bottom drawer.

Immediately she could remember her old abandoned clothes, what she wore when she wasn't in school uniform. She raised the edge of each folded item a couple of inches, looking through the piles to see if there was anything she still wanted. Mostly sweaters and jeans she wore on the farm. Aimee realized she was searching for clothes from her early childhood. Wanting to see clothes she wore when her mother was alive, vests and blouses her mother washed and ironed. Could there possibly be such items still around?

Aimee walked to the closet and slid the door open. The top shelf had extra blankets and pillows. Only a few hangers held any clothing. The closet was mostly empty. Aimee wandered to her parents' room, her father's room. It was already nine in the morning and her dad and Colin would be nearly done feeding the cows and mucking the stalls.

The bed had a brass frame with a white eyelet bedspread. Her father had neatly made it at five-thirty that morning. She'd known that bedspread since infancy. She'd been propped, like a tripod, on the quilt before she could walk, pushing tiny finger-tips through the lace holes, while her mother sang to her from the shower or folded clothes beside her on the bed. Standing there, Aimee realized her father must periodically wash the coverlet by hand to have preserved it this long, and she could see at a glance that he was ironing it too. Aimee sat on the side of the bed, letting her hands caress the texture of the eyelet. The mattress was too soft. Instinctually she knew this would be the same mattress they bought as newlyweds, thirty-five years ago. The same mattress Pauline had conceived five children on. Aimee was pretty sure her oldest brother, Jack Jr., was born at home. Most likely on this bed.

By the time Aimee came along, her brothers were 13, 11, 10, and 8 years old. And they were her father's domain and additional farm hands when they weren't in school. Aimee was the only girl in the family. Her mother, Pauline, was forty-four at her birth. She was also many years a drinker. All of this had contributed to Aimee being her mother's charge, separated by age and gender from her brothers and father. And she grew to be a necessary anchor, to keep her mother from drifting off to sea.

Aimee could clearly remember the suffocating love and attention of her mother. Love she could feel like a heavy child on her lap, and smell like the sickly sweet smell of booze. She was seven when her mother died on the couch in front of the TV while everyone else slept. And although Aimee grieved and suffered survivor's guilt, she didn't miss her mother. What washed over her, as she sat on her parents' bed, having been on the farm for five days, having been away from the farm for almost five years, having been away from Ireland for half a year, felt more like missing her mother than anything she had ever felt before.

Aimee was surprised to hear her own voice, full of sorrow. And more surprised by the words that floated into the room. "What can I do for yer, Mum?"

Before leaving her parents' room, she opened their closet as well. Like ghosts, she found several of Pauline's dresses hanging off to one side. Right away she could see they were her size. She'd never thought about being the same stature as her mother now that she was grown. Aimee was short and petite, as her mother had been.

The dresses were not special. They were what her mum called housedresses, with pockets, one plaid, one a solid olive green, one a dusky rose color. Aimee handled each one, and held the green one against her body, turning toward the mirror above her father's dresser.

Behind her reflection she saw her father standing in the doorway.

"You scared the hell out of me." She shrieked.

"My room." Her dad replied. "The farrier is here to trim hooves. Thought you could lend a calming hand. Since you slept through chores this morning."

"Sure." Aimee put the dress back into the closet.

"She'd be right proud to see you now."

Aimee couldn't remember the last time her dad referenced her mum. It had been many years. Her throat constricted.

"Push my suit aside. There's her one gown. The blue one. She wore that at your confirmation. I guess it's out of style now; still elegant to me."

Aimee touched the midnight-blue satin hesitantly, as though it might grab her fingertips. It was not out of style, it was classic. She wanted to try it on. She wanted it as her own. Aimee realized she possessed nothing that had belonged to her mother.

Her father may have read her thoughts. "If you fancy it, it's yours. It's just hanging there, of no use to me."

"I'll try it on. It looks so small."

"She was a size 4, figure just like yours until she got a bit older." Jack O'Malley sighed. Pauline didn't get very old, Aimee understood.

It was not a practical matter, the dress. It didn't matter if Aimee wore it ever, or if it was in-style. She wanted her mother's one good dress.

"Thank you, Dad. I'd like to 'ave it."

—

Aimee was reading in her room, after having packed her mother's dress in her suitcase, when she abruptly had the desire to call Connor. If there was someone from her youth who she really talked to, it was him. She went to find Colin downstairs.

"You have a phone number for Connor?"

Without answering her, he picked up his cellphone, scrolled through his contacts, and then handed the device up to her. "Tell him happy new year from me."

Aimee carried the cell phone back to her room, held gingerly in her fingertips. Once she was back on her bed with her textbooks spread out around her, she pressed his number. The bedroom, the books and calling Connor were suddenly a reenactment of the past.

Connor picked up, "Hey, Colin."

"No, it's me, Aimee."

"Wow. Hey, Aimee. Hold on a second…"

She realized that he was probably with Margaret. They probably lived together. It struck her as good of him that he'd said her name out loud. This was no clandestine phone call.

His familiar voice came back on the line. "How are you?"

"Grand. Little funny to be home, but nice. Been too long, I guess. My dad's getting older." She said that for no reason. He didn't seem any older to her.

"Yeah. I'm a bit surprised to hear from you, to be honest."

"Me too." Aimee laughed nervously. "Colin told me you're getting married. And I've seen Margaret. I'm happy for you both. I wanted to say hello and congratulations."

"Thanks Aimee. Margaret told me. So you staying in New York? Is that the place for you?"

It chilled Aimee to be asked that. It was like others had always wondered what was the place for her.

"Aye. I like New York. Who knows?"

"Hey. You want to come to our wedding? If you're still in town New Year's Eve."

"Wow. Aye, I'm still here. It's my last night actually."

"Five o'clock, St. Paul's Church. The reception is at Fels Point Hotel."

Aimee did not want to attend Connor's wedding. She was looking for something else; she suddenly knew that what she wanted was to get a drink or a meal with Connor alone. To discuss with him what her youth had really been like. Was it possible that Connor could help her see where she came from? Attending Connor's wedding to Margaret was not the connection she was longing for. But she had just said yes.

"Well, if I can ..." but Connor had already rung off.

—

Aimee wore her mother's one good dress to Connor's wedding. She drove herself to the ceremony in the jeep. It wasn't until she climbed the church steps and saw Connor's parents in a receiving line that she thought Connor's secondary school girlfriend, however distant, coming to his wedding from America, might be classified as a spectacle in Castlemaine.

His mother put her mind at ease, squeezing Aimee's hands with real affection, and saying, "My, you've grown into a woman, lass. So good of you to come." Connor's father nodded at her with a scowl. The dress was too low in the chest and too tight on her hips, and she had grown into a woman.

Connor stood with friends in the back of the church, greeting his guests as they arrived. Margaret was presumably sequestered in a church room, with her mother, or sisters, or close friends fussing over her gown, her veil. Aimee had a flash thought that she would never be the bride at a wedding, Catholic or otherwise. Who would dress her, Dad in his overalls?

The sight of Connor in a black tuxedo, filled out considerably from his twenty-year-old physique, his boyish contagious smile, was a shock. He was unnaturally handsome. She had forgotten.

When he saw Aimee standing just inside the church's large wooden doors, looking his way, he kept his ear bent to his friend's talk, and the same smile held in place, but his eyes were intensely focused on her. She waved, but then stepped in the opposite direction, out of Connor's sightline. She wished she'd eaten before coming, suddenly feeling light-headed.

Aimee did not get a chance to greet Connor before the ceremony. The Catholic priest was one she'd never seen before, but her family didn't attend church. She'd heard nearly identical wedding sermons before, but still it startled her to have Christ directly referred to as a being, and to hear the about-to-be-wed couple warned against sin.

While Aimee watched, seated alone beside Connor's uncle and aunt, she had an unreasonable wish that Connor would turn around and look for her in the audience during the ceremony. He did not. He lifted Margaret's veil revealing her tight red curls; her brown eyes briefly reminded Aimee of the cows, wet and trusting eyes. Connor kissed Margaret, both hands around her head. Had he kissed her that same way? They had spent so many hours kissing; a teenage life with so much free time and prudish restrictions, that kissing could last for a couple of hours a day. She thought unexpectedly of her parents, who she had never seen share a single kiss.

Connor began lowering the veil over Margaret's face again. She shook her head at him and quietly laughed. He laughed too, and carefully secured it behind her head and falling down her shoulders. They came back down the aisle together to exit the church before their guests. From somewhere in the room, an organ began to be played. Everyone stood. This time Aimee felt that Connor's eyes intentionally did not find her standing four steps in from the aisle.

The reception was a five-minute walk away. Aimee followed the crowd there. She felt out of place. Where were the people she knew? She wondered if she could skip the dinner, congratulate them both and leave within an hour. Once in the hotel's banquet room, she was approached by a waiter with a tray of Champagne flutes. She took one and drank it in two sips. Suddenly, she was encircled by a group of her old secondary school friends. Here were the friends she'd gone to the cinema with, or prowled around the shopping centre with, swam with in every local lake, and tasted first drinks and puffs of cigarettes together.

"Aimee!" She saw two brunettes heading towards her, Hilary and Abby. Aimee had run track with them every day after school. She felt her own face lighting up. Why had she not stayed in touch with them? The young women hugged and filled each other in on their lives in surprisingly few words.

A couple of the guys from her youth, who were broader in their shoulders and whose faces had filled out too, flirted immediately. It was innocent fun. Aimee's mood became light. She drank two more Champagnes in secession and flirted back. She jabbered about life in New York City and a bit about her college years in Dublin, and the guys skirted around the subjects of their local jobs, more than one in farming, and their imminent plans for marriage too. Quite a few were already married or engaged, there was a pregnancy and new baby spoken of too. Aimee began looking forward to dinner and dancing now. She wanted to keep messing around with old friends, harmlessly flirting with the guys, and enjoying the giddy sensation of alcohol in her veins. Her imminent departure from Ireland opened a portal of freedom that ran through her.

Finally Connor and Margaret entered the banquet hall. They moved about the room, greeting family members and friends. Margaret was bombarded for moments of female bonding, twice as long as Connor's quick shoulder-pound embraces. The newlyweds drifted apart in the room, being congratulated. Aimee tried not to watch Connor's progress through the room. But each time she did look, he was taking a glass of Champagne off a moving tray. She took another one too, even though she heard her words slur as she told a joke. She felt her mother in her very facial muscles, the crooked laughter and the alcohol.

The next thing she knew, Connor's mouth was next to her ear. He stood somehow out of her sight, just a disembodied voice. "Aimee, Aimee. You've come back. To my wedding."

Aimee turned to face him. "Congratulations, Connor."

"Indeed." He looked for the white dress and red hair and after spotting her, said, "I'm a lucky man." Connor grabbed another Champagne glass and thrust it at Aimee, took another for himself. "I just want to tell you one thing. Come with me." He didn't pull her hand, just walked away.

She quickly followed. "Where are we going?"

"Nowhere. I just want someplace we can talk for one minute."

They turned several corners and the noise from the banquet hall almost disappeared. They were in a dark-paneled vestibule.

"Why'd you do it, Aimee?"

"What?"

"Why'd you have sex with me? Why'd you lose your virginity with me and break up with me ten minutes later? Why didn't you save it? Maybe not for your husband, but for someone you truly loved?"

This might have been the conversation Aimee had wanted when she'd called Connor. To figure out who that girl had been, and thus to learn who she was now and who she was becoming. But she didn't want to hear these words from him here, drunker than she should be, and at his wedding. She felt obliged to try to answer him, since she'd never given an explanation.

"I wanted someone experienced to show me. I wanted it to be you. I just didn't want to be your girlfriend anymore." Aimee's timidity felt just like the night she had ended their relationship.

Connor laughed harshly. "You always sound so sane. I wasn't experienced. I was a virgin too."

"Oh, Connor, I'm sorry. It was so long ago."

Connor wasn't listening. His face wore an expression she remembered, the enthrall of concentration she would see when he worked on his jeep's engine. First she thought he was nine years back in his room, on his bed, seeing her black cotton underwear and white bra. But then she saw he was in the present, dangerously in the present.

"Look at this," he murmured appreciatively. "Who knew this was here." He pulled open a narrow, painted black door. Once the door was open, an elevator door rattled open within it. Inside was a dark wooden elevator box the size of a coat closet.

"It's like a dumbwaiter."

Connor was holding the elevator open while he spoke, staring into it. Aimee was about to say they should go back to the party, when Connor picked up her hand. "Shite," he whispered, as he stepped in, leading her in behind him.

The door shut and Connor pushed '2.' As the elevator rose, he pushed the STOP button, causing the box to shudder to a stop.

"Let's have sex in here. Because it was only the once, with no proper ending. Now, it'll be only the once, but it'll end it all."

"Connor." But Aimee was shocked by her own want.

Connor stroked her shoulders, under the straps of the blue dress. He leaned in and kissed her. "It was always so amazing to kiss you and touch you. I think about the time we had sex more than you'd know."

Aimee kissed him back. "Hurry, Connor. Now."

Connor slid her dress up around her waist. He lifted her feet, one at a time to slip the underwear off over her high heels. He began to shove her underwear in his pocket.

"No! Leave it on the floor."

He dropped her underwear and undid his belt and let his tuxedo pants fall to the floor. Then he lifted Aimee and pressed her into the wall of the tiny elevator. She wrapped her legs around his waist. His back nearly touched the opposite wall. In a second he was inside her. They rocked and kissed. She felt his strong hips behind her thighs. She felt his arms supporting her full weight and she knew when he was going to come. She had not realized that she was too, until she did. They came quickly and at the same time, the way she'd imagined it would happen eight years ago, when she was fifteen. Connor put her down and she pulled on her own underwear. When he'd straightened his clothes, she looked at him for any signs of what had happened.

"Luckily I left all my lipstick on Champagne glasses."

Connor nodded curtly and released the STOP button.

"Connor. You two will be very happy. She's great."

"She *is* great. I love her. Please believe that."

"I know you do."

They parted at the elevator with a scared moment of eye contact and no parting words.

Aimee looked into the ballroom at Connor and Margaret's guests. They laughed, or danced, or talked at tables. They had not noticed anything amiss. She looked around desperately for an exit. Nearly blind with shock and self-loathing, she pushed through an exit door. Aimee walked with her head down in search of where she'd left the jeep. She was horrified to see she weaved as she walked, but not sympathetic to herself or concerned for her safety. *Why in the world did I come to Ireland and do this?*

An invisible wire guided the jeep back to the farm. Or like one of their escaped cattle, Aimee had inexplicable homing skills. Aimee imagined driving the jeep into a ravine. *Is this feeling suicidal?* She arrived home unscathed and stumbled into the kitchen and read the wall clock above the stove. 11:50 p.m. She stepped out of the high heel shoes and opened the fridge. She grabbed a glass bottle of fresh milk and drank it in huge gulps. Standing in front of the open fridge, she ate cold chicken with her fingers, wanting the food to make her drunkenness go away. She felt sore from the sex, and she remembered the pleasure, making her cringe in shame. She thought of Margaret. Then she looked down at her body in her mother's gown. *I'm leaving Ireland in a matter of hours.*

The overhead light flipped on.

"You're home early. How was the wedding?" Her dad stood in the doorway in his pajamas, smiling at her.

Aimee spun around from the refrigerator, her lips greasy with chicken, her hands raised to her mouth.

There was something in her expression that caused her father's blood to run cold, that brought a frightened look to his face. Aimee thought, *he's seen a ghost.*

"You're drunk."

"Why didn't you help her?" Aimee shouted.

"Mum?" Her father's voice was barely audible.

"Yes, Mum! Why'd you let her kill herself? Why'd you stand by and watch her grow sicker and sicker? And she was in charge of me!"

Jack O'Malley had dealt with blood and tears and dirt and shit and birth and death his whole life. The earthly elements, the stuff of animals was what he knew. And although he looked stunned by her accusation, her rage and drunkenness, he was capable of handling it.

"I didn't know how to stop her. It's not how we do things here, Aimee. There was no help I knew of. And you were her lass. Yer Mama kept you close. Aimee, you can't come visit all these years later and blame me."

He'd said come visit and not come home. This wasn't Aimee's home anymore, had it ever been? Aimee threw the drumstick she held towards her father. She wiped her filthy hands on her stomach, smearing grease on the satin dress.

"She was your wife, and she was drinking herself to death, and you did nothing to help her. Am I an American now if I think people should intervene when their wife is an alcoholic? You didn't try to stop her, and I couldn't do anything—I couldn't do anything but watch her go. She died from lack of love, because love is interfering!"

Aimee ran past her father, sobbing. Nothing she said was a known thought to her. Every word was a new and foreign grievance, something that lay deeply buried within her, that was unleashed by barely known forces.

10.

JONATHAN AND Theo were spending Christmas Eve and Christmas Day on Long Island at his sister Emily's home. This year, Carly had Thanksgiving and he had Christmas; the next year they would switch. Carly had dropped by on the morning of Christmas Eve, before Jonathan drove out to Long Island, to see Theo and give Jonathan a few presents to bring out there from her. She handed him a small silver-wrapped box, "Give this to Emily for me please."

"Thanks, Carly. That's really thoughtful of you." He meant it. Thoughtfulness was one of Carly's many graces.

"Say hello to everyone for me. Oh, are you wrapping something from Santa?"

Jonathan shook his head at this charade that somehow continued to get him and Carly each year. "I did. Some interactive books and a Snoopy. I can't seem to resist the magical thinking."

"Good. Magical thinking is good for you." She'd already hugged and kissed Theo. She squeezed Jonathan's arm and slipped out of the apartment.

Jonathan had seen Sara a few days before Christmas, before they both left on their respective holiday plans. She would be visiting family on the West Coast for the holiday. They'd exchanged gifts in his bed, with a combination of tenderness and shyness. Jonathan sensed that she too didn't know what level of intimacy she wished to convey in this first exchange of Christmas presents. They'd each bought the other a book, in the end. He wasn't disappointed in the seemingly non-romantic present. And she'd chosen just right for him, a photographic history of the skyscrapers of New York, called "1,000 New York Buildings." Miraculously, he didn't own it already. He had bought her a trilogy of novels from a prominent Brazilian novelist. The books had just been re-released as a box set with a beautiful red and white graphic design, a neat little package that was a pleasure to handle. He liked that Sara loved reading novels. He himself only read non-fiction.

There'd been an air of parting between them that was outsized for the occasion. It must have been the holiday itself and the impending new year. And Jonathan and Sara would be entering a new year as a couple. He felt unequivocally that their feelings were matched on this subject. There was so much sweetness around their stolen hours together.

Christmas Eve at his sister's house was the reliable ritual he knew it would be. He'd shared many holidays with Emily, Brad and their two kids, Sophia and Emmett. After the three children were all asleep on Christmas Eve, Jonathan, Emily, and Brad, each with glasses of red wine, began stuffing stockings and arranging presents under the tree.

Emily held up a box wrapped in candy-cane paper. "This is a 3-D puzzle for Theo. Its super cool and meant to increase fine motor skills."

"I'm sure he'll love it."

"Well, now that I've spent some time with him, I'm afraid the puzzle is too easy." Emily said, frowning at the wrapped gift.

This was the first visit where Theo followed behind his two cousins, keeping pace, in a wheelchair. The ground floor of the house could be circuited through a swinging door between the kitchen and dining room, crossing the foyer into a den, through French doors to the living room and back into the kitchen. The three children made this loop over and over again. Sophia ran backwards, cheering for Theo as he steered EZ at top speeds from tile to wood to carpet, his cousins beaming faces mirroring his.

—

The following afternoon, after the frenzy of opening too many gifts, the grown-ups sipping coffee and Bloody Mary's, Jonathan sat on the couch with his phone in his hand. He opened his email. He hadn't seen the name Aimee O'Malley in his email since their exchange prior to her arrival in America, settling all the details of her employment.

This missive was a sweet and quirky greeting, with no other purpose than reminding him to give Theo a favorite treat, yogurt with maple syrup. Perhaps because he himself was tipsy, he imagined Aimee was tipsy too when she'd written him a Christmas greeting from Ireland. For the first time, he contemplated what her alcohol or even recreational drug use might be, being merely twenty-three years old. Maybe it was the Irish-Catholic upbringing, or just pure Aimee, but she struck him as a very sober young person. She was too damn ardent in life and school and all her convictions, to be one to willingly go for loss of control, was his guess.

"Merry Christmas, to the best nanny in County Kerry ..." Jonathan deleted the words and started over. "Merry Christmas, Aimee! Theo's very well, but no doubt is missing you. See you soon." He added a smiley face emoji just like she had.

Many things were shifting for Jonathan as of late. His romantic relationship with Sara, which continued to surprise and delight him. His hugely improved relationship with Carly, their returned bond and respect, love in fact. And most significantly, what he thought of as Theo's super-acceleration, Theo reading, Theo maneuvering about in his wheelchair. Theo's new progress coincided with Aimee's presence in their lives. Aimee herself was another shift in their lives. Yet he didn't entirely attribute to Aimee what felt like an organic developmental leap in his son.

Their lives were undergoing change, more change than they'd had in years, and he couldn't help but feel there was something cosmic about it. Jonathan thought of the Big Bang. He also wondered about readiness. Being ready and change occurring, was a chicken and the egg. He was ready to fall in love with Sara. He was ready to be challenged by Aimee. He was ready for the world to meet Theo as he was. And most importantly, all that readiness was the atmosphere in which Theo was able to burst forth. He understood how people spoke of the universe opening to an idea or an event.

Also tantamount on Jonathan's mind was the introduction of Theo and Sara that was planned for Thursday night. He anxiously awaited this moment. The idea of introducing them magnified his feelings for each of them. Theo, the center of his life, his life's purpose, and Sara, who was stirring in him the most romantic feelings he'd had in over ten years. He knew they were going to get along. He could see it already in his mind's eye.

Without meaning to, he kept picturing Sara and Theo engaged in different activities. Playing on the floor in his living room would be the first to actually happen. But he was also

imagining them on a boat, on a beach, in Paris. He squashed
these thoughts the moment he registered them, but he allowed
himself the brief happiness they brought on.

—

On Thursday night, Jonathan cooked a pork loin. He rolled
the log of pork in a spice rub of cumin, cinnamon, salt, black
pepper, cayenne and brown sugar. He would put it in the oven
after Sara arrived. He had left work early to meet Theo at the
school bus, then vacuum, tidy up, and make dinner for the three
of them. Aimee would be in Ireland until the following week.

Jonathan left the kitchen, drying his hands on an apron. Theo
was coloring on the living room floor. He wore a red shirt and
black jogger jeans, part of the updated wardrobe Jonathan had
recently bought him. He viewed Theo objectively for an instant,
the first impression he'd make on Sara. The frozen image of his
son morphed into a Carly painting as well. His legs mermaided
to the side, the sunlight falling on him and the reds and blues
of his oriental rug.

He looked at his watch. It was six on the nose. He sat on the
couch and picked up the magazine from last Sunday's paper. As
he neared the end of an article on the increase of recreational
spaces in NYC, he realized Sara was quite late. His phone was
beside him on the couch, and he knew without looking that she
hadn't texted. Irritability flickered through him. He looked at
his watch, almost 6:40 p.m.

Theo rose onto his hands and knees and crawled to him. He
placed his hands on the couch, kneeling. "What's for eat?"

Jonathan didn't need his boy sensing his frustration. The
evening felt thwarted already, he felt quite certain of this. He
had told Theo that a friend was coming for dinner. It was past

the time they usually ate. If Theo had forgotten their intended guest, there was no need to remind him.

"I'm going to put the pork in the oven. Okay? Dinner in half an hour."

Theo nodded his head vigorously. "I'm hungry."

It was almost for Theo's sake that he texted Sara. He wanted smoothness. It was Sara's responsibility to inform him she was late, but as he stood to go to the oven, he fired off, *Everything okay? Dinner's going in the o----*, he stopped and deleted the dinner part, sent it and slipped the phone in his pocket, resentful that he now felt he was waiting for her reply.

He had a strong sense that Sara wasn't coming. And although he didn't typically view his nightly dinners with Theo as precious moments of family time, he longed for the normalcy of cooking a meal for himself and Theo and sitting down to eat it without a single stressful thought or feeling. There was a reason dating hadn't ranked high as a priority these past three years. He wanted peace.

For fifteen minutes, while he mixed a green salad, roasted asparagus with the pork on the top broiler shelf, and set the table, still for three, he alternated between phantom hearing the doorbell and the certainty that she wasn't coming, nor calling. He was perplexed, mentally reevaluating the past four and a half months. The many moments that love seemed to be actually taking root, and yet she was becoming a stranger again by the second.

He wished dinner wasn't almost ready. It seemed that despite his ambivalence, his cooking was on a speed course to completion and then consumption. He wanted to give her a little more time.

With the entire meal ready and on the counter, Jonathan stared at his phone. How could it be 7:00 p.m., an hour late, and no word?

"Theo, let's eat!"

Jonathan pulled the third setting off the table, and served himself and Theo slices of pork loin, asparagus, and salad. He pushed his phone, upside down, behind the fruit bowl, and cut Theo's pork into bite-size pieces. Theo ate them with his fingers immediately.

"Good, huh? I love you, Bunny."

He poured himself wine.

Halfway through dinner the phone vibrated. His hand jumped but he didn't look. He finished the somewhat false conversation he was having with Theo and finally reached for the phone.

I'm so sorry. Can I meet you tomorrow to explain?

He wanted none of the anger, confusion, disgust, relief, fear, or tenderness that was a wild swirl within him. There was no rush to reply, that he was sure of. He got up to stash the phone on his desk in the other room. He needed to make this night his and Theo's again.

Before Jonathan went to bed, he texted Sara.

I'll be going to the Jetson early tomorrow. I can meet you at 10:00 a.m.

He was careful to not phrase his message as a question. He powered down his phone, knowing he had to prevent obsessively waiting for more messages. While he brushed and flossed his teeth and tidied his bedroom before bed, he felt gratitude for the domestic fortress he'd created in the past few years for Theo and himself. He drew up the drawbridge.

—

Jonathan worked for two hours at the site before going to meet Sara, willfully focused on work. He stayed in conversation with his foreman, the electricians, and the carpenters almost continuously, compartmentalizing his many ill-feelings about Sara.

She was there when he arrived, and he sat beside her on a barstool facing the street without getting a coffee. He didn't speak and she didn't either for a moment.

"I'm really sorry about last night. It was incredibly rude. Jonathan, there's no good way to put this, I'm getting married."

Jonathan outwardly took this news like a statue. It made sense. His mind raced to dozens of moments between them, framing his memories inside this new information. His mind played a trick on him as well—he half thought she was broaching the subject of marriage between the two of them. His thoughts also contained a swift-motion play of that conversation, his saying he loved her, but was nowhere near ready to consider marriage. Alas, he'd considered love from the moment he talked to her on the goddamn beams, tattered summer clouds behind her head.

"I feel absolutely horrible. It was just awful of me not to tell you about this. Right before we met, I broke off my engagement with my fiancé. The thing was, we were broken up, but I think I really knew we weren't. A severe case of cold feet." *'Right before we met.'* Jonathan could pinpoint the moment they met; she'd dropped her cellphone into her pocket like she wanted to discard the caller on the other end. He'd been a fool. "I hardly spoke to him at all this whole time. But last week, we spoke endlessly, we tore everything apart. I don't need to tell you about that, how unfair. But I'm getting married. I'm engaged again, with a date, and I can't see you anymore, obviously."

Jonathan stared out the window at the pedestrians hurrying by on Twenty-First Street. He did not want to see Sara's face. He'd come to know it very well. He knew her eyes would look faintly pinched with the anguish of the conversation. Her wrinkleless face, her skin that was often dewy and at times showed tiny pores, and in certain lights, the white peach fuzz that grew where he had sideburns.

"Jonathan, I'm so sorry. I feel like this must happen with men much more than women—that there's someone else. I'm not making any excuses for myself."

He turned to face her, bitterness rising in his throat. "Oh, yes. And if *I* was actually engaged, and you went around telling your friends, there'd be knowing eye-rolls all around. '*Oh, men.*' You're the asshole, Sara." He was so grateful she hadn't touched Theo, they hadn't laid eyes on each other or shared space. He almost voiced those things to her, but what would be the point?

"I deserve your anger. But this wasn't a lie. I want you to know that. I really enjoyed the time we spent together. I was falling for you and having a great time. But you and I were never talking about the future. I don't think I led you on. I hope not."

There was no need to talk about any of it anymore. There was a distant thought heading toward him, a blurry epiphany. Sara had been able to take him less seriously as a partner, able to disregard him even, because he was a father. His life, totally encumbered by caring for his disabled son, was somehow less touchable, less affect-able, safely entrenched from a romantic relationship. His life gave Sara some unconscious permission to not worry about her impact on his future. It was vague, and not something he was going to explore in the moment, but it shed some dim light on his situation, on their whole entanglement and her swift exit from it.

He stood. His hands in his pockets, his eyes outside, "Take care, Sara." He left.

As he walked down the sidewalk, the first day this winter that gloves were called for, he realized that he and Sara had not exchanged a single text, call or email over the Christmas holiday. She was not visiting family on the West Coast, as she had said. She was with her fiancé, reconciling.

It was New Year's Eve, a fact he had not registered since Sara had not shown up for dinner. Theo would be at Carly's for the night. He had a dinner reservation for two at a restaurant in Williamsburg at 9 p.m. They'd had dinner plans, he and Sara. Did she even remember that? While he walked in the general direction of the Jetson, he took out his phone to cancel it.

—

On Aimee's first day back from Ireland, Jonathan let her in at 7:00 a.m. as usual, ready to get to his morning routine. But he slowed his pace a beat noticing some shift in Aimee, some elemental change beneath her skin, something raw.

"How was your trip?"

"Glad to be back, actually."

Theo appeared behind Jonathan with an abrupt braking of EZ. He yelped with delight, matching that of a surprise party, at seeing Aimee. "Mee-Mee!"

Jonathan observed Aimee's demeanor change. "Theo! I missed you so much."

Aimee sidled up to Theo's wheelchair and gripped him around one shoulder. The two cooed and murmured like doves.

While still hugging Theo, Aimee asked, "And how are you faring?"

"I've been all right." Jonathan said flatly.

The two exchanged a long glance, as though they could each see some emotional wear-and-tear in the other.

When Jonathan returned home that evening, Aimee greeted him with, "The 9th Street Y will take the staircase. They can pick it up tomorrow."

Jonathan looked past Aimee's shoulder at the blue foam staircase that she'd brought into their home months ago, that had aggravated him to no end. That day was before so much. Before reading, before knowing about Carly's paintings, before EZ, before Sara, and other murkier things, like his deepened trust in Aimee herself. And now she was saying it was time to get rid of it. Although the staircase was merely an object, obtrusive, and ugly, and recently unused, it had grown into a symbol of all he must give up in the name of growth. He found some objects did this to him. Put rawness in his throat, as though the objects were replicas of Carly leaving him, of Sara deceiving him, of the original pain and loss of Theo "leaving" by changing from one child into another child. Jonathan had seen Theo's regression this way for a long time, like the disappearance of his Theo. The idea felt unstable now, like a thing dissolving. Jonathan could almost grasp that his thinking was wrong, as he looked at Theo furiously coloring a whale blue in a coloring book. There'd been no disappearance. But Jonathan held onto his pain. It belonged to him too.

"Yeah. He's done with it." Jonathan admitted mournfully.

"You want to keep it?"

"No, it just seems to mark an important era, and now the end of an era. A lot has happened in the time of the staircase." Jonathan said aloud but almost to himself.

"I guess that's what stairs do. They take you up."

"Or down." Jonathan felt a dark emotion pour over him, as though a cauldron had lowered and drowned him in its foul contents. It was self-pity, he recognized it almost from outside himself–*so this is what self-pity feels like*–the emotion pure and clean. But the recognition of the emotion wasn't enough to take it away. It stuffed his very soul with what he felt he'd lost, as opposed to anyone else. He had been dealt a very bad hand. His son had been changed. He had been forced to let that fourteen-month-old baby go. That Theo was gone. And his disappearance had taken Jonathan's wife with it. Like a tsunami had whisked his family from his arms. And his friendships and career became shells of what they were. His joy shriveled. Sara had brought joy and renewal, but it had been all untrue, an illusion. He was drowning in self-pity. He tried to grasp the one thought that felt like his future. He hadn't lost Theo. His boy was still alive and well. So many had suffered worse. So many *had* lost their children. Theo was here. But Jonathan couldn't climb out of his darkness yet.

"You brought it in, and you can give it away. You're the decision-maker around here, Aimee." Jonathan made a shooing gesture with his hands that spoke to the staircase and to Aimee at once.

Jonathan knew that Aimee saw this dark change come over him. He saw her hands ball into fists.

"You could be a fecking Irish for all your stiff upper-lipping, your stoic front. You're feeling pissy about something?"

"Yeah. I can feel pissy."

Aimee scowled. "Get off it. Since I've known Theo, he's made years-worth of progress in a few months. You want something more? Grand. Fight for it. And refuse to stop getting better. Don't blame me. And never think Theo aihn't working 'ard! Look in the mirror."

Aimee picked up her backpack and headed for the door. "You want to keep the stairs? You don't effing need them anymore."

All Jonathan could manage was to shake his head no.

"Grand." Aimee left.

Jonathan looked at the closed door for a long time.

—

After Aimee had gone, Jonathan looked through the fridge for what he might cook for dinner. Theo appeared in the kitchen. He'd changed into his pajamas by himself. He no longer slept in a diaper. Just a seven year old in his pajamas, sitting on the kitchen floor.

"Hey, Boomer, what if I make pancakes and bacon for dinner? Would that be fun?"

"Breakfast for dinner!" Theo shouted.

"It's a thing. Want to help me make the batter?"

"Yes. I stir." Theo headed towards his chair at the table where he sometimes helped cook. "Bring bowl, Dada, and the eggs."

"Yes, Sir."

Jonathan brought over the flour, baking powder, salt, and sugar. He placed everything in Theo's reach.

"You and Mee-Mee fight."

Jonathan thought about denying it. "Yes. Sometimes grownups argue, but they can still be friends. I was wrong."

"Dada is wrong." Theo said happily. "Need measure cup and measure spoon." He pointed toward the kitchen drawers where they were kept. "Bring, please."

Jonathan was happy to oblige.

After Theo was in bed, Jonathan laid an 11 x 24 rendering of the Jetson on the dining table. It was a clean rendition of the structure with the two "green" augmentations he'd decided to keep: solar panels on the main roof and a living roof adjacent to the 16th floor terrace. Impulsively and automatically, he began labelling the dimensions with pencil, adding the footage of every parallel and perpendicular intersection by memory. He knew what the flex needed to be for every fourth story off the ground and the cubic weight of the counterbalances in the top four stories. The very engineering that made skyscrapers stand up and stay up. He jotted those numbers in the margins. He had three sharpened pencils on the table.

He got up and poured a scotch and put on Ella Fitzgerald. When he returned to the table, he chose a new pencil, and he drew a fox peering out from behind the Jetson. Then he drew a raccoon, standing on its hind legs off to the side. In an upper window, he drew an owl. He had been a skillful artist from the time he was in kindergarten, but he had not drawn like this since he was eleven years old. He had never made an unrelated mark on a blueprint before. He began singing along with Ella, while he added stars.

11.

Jonathan called Carly early in the morning, upon waking. While the thought was fresh and before he could second guess it, he asked her. "What do you think about Theo having another comprehensive assessment?"

"I...don't...know, Jonathan," she said with air between every word. "No one has suggested it. But I was wondering about it myself—actually. I know that's surprising."

Carly's thoughts were surprising due to the fact that she had never wanted the first one. Their disagreement had cemented a wedge that had pushed between them.

"It's been over three years since his last assessment."

They both knew exactly how long it had been. Three years and eight months. The length of time they had been separated.

He would forever link that three-day assessment with Carly asking for the separation. She had asked for the separation the night they'd been given the devastating results.

Jonathan pressed on into this dangerous territory. "I feel its time."

"Okay. Let's ask Dr. Wyatt. How was Theo's night?" Carly asked.

"Fine. He's good. We baked."

"You okay, Jonathan?"

Jonathan rubbed his hair. He was still in bed, having called her immediately upon waking. "Sure. I'm okay."

—

Jonathan and Carly met in front of Mt. Sinai West on 10th Avenue to go into the appointment together. A week earlier, Theo had endured a four-day evaluation and assessment. He'd conducted a marathon of mental and physical obstacle courses, to determine his current stage of gross and fine motor skills, speech, cognitive capacity, analytical reasoning, sight, hearing; his entire being tested.

On this day, they'd get the results explained to them by Dr. Wyatt, Theo's neurologist. The first intensive evaluation since he was four, when they were informed that his encephalitis was determined to have a permanent effect on his brain.

The evening of that assessment's results, three years earlier, Carly had uttered her inability to go on. Appearing as incredulous as Jonathan felt hearing her, she said she had to move out, get away from this household. The evaluation results left her freefalling. Literally, she felt the ground beneath her was gone. A sensation of continuous falling persisted for hours, so that she lay on the floor to save her life. And the one image that came to her of solid ground, was a separate apartment to fall in.

When he called Emily in stunned grief to say that Carly was moving out, she said: "You shouldn't have done that evaluation. Carly wasn't ready for it. It could have waited. She's devastated."

Jonathan replied, "I didn't think our marriage hung on it."

Now again, they were waiting together to learn the results of Theo's second comprehensive evaluation. This time as a separated couple.

Carly rubbed her palms on her thighs as she sat in a hard chair beside Jonathan in the doctor's waiting room. She almost always wore jeans, and Jonathan noticed what nice legs she had, he'd always thought so.

"God, I'm nervous. Are you?" Carly asked.

"I don't know, not really. How so?" They were both whispering.

"I'm terrified he will be exactly the same. To be honest, I'm too sure that he's different. I wish I had no expectations."

"It will be different."

Carly looked surprised.

"He's seven. People change over time. He's being re-evaluated after three years. He's changed so much even these past six months."

Suddenly, Carly began sobbing. She pressed into Jonathan's shoulder, hiding her face. He stroked her back, as it convulsed beneath his hand. He glanced at the one other couple in the waiting room, who discreetly did not look at Carly or him. He no longer wondered if she'd forgotten that it was on the tail of Theo's first evaluation, with the results of permanent damage, that she'd walked out of their lives. Did Carly think Theo's fate was told in these tests?

With each stroke of her back, he tried to convey that it was not that.

"When we see the stars in the sky, Carly, it's just the illumination they shed light years ago. They're gone now, they're dead or faded or elsewhere, they're not the perfectly clear and real-seeming view we see so vividly. His assessment is just how Theo was doing last week, when they ran him through test after test. It's light that was shed from the galaxy of his brain a week ago, already moving on somewhere else. We can't capture Theo's intelligence and potential from any test. He's on the move each day."

Carly raised her face, inches in front of his. Her black bangs were pressed into her forehead, damp at her temples, her blue eyes were bloodshot from sudden forceful tears and they were incredulous. Her mouth parted but no words came.

Jonathan kissed her very quickly on the lips.

Carly moved her head away in surprise. Jonathan felt the same surprise, which they both chose to dismiss.

"I've never, ever heard you speak that way before." Carly's expression made Jonathan laugh out loud.

"Brooks." The receptionist called.

They both rose at once, and they turned to head into the offices, still connected, Jonathan's arm slung tight around Carly's shoulder.

Dr. Wyatt pushed identical papers toward each of them. Theo's report based on all the findings. Her brisk movements somehow indicated good news. Jonathan didn't have his bearings yet; he couldn't begin reading and the words swam away from his vision while he thought of his boy. But Carly jolted in her seat and grabbed his hand that rested on his thigh. He squeezed her hand back and waited to be told what was now the state of Theo.

"So," said Dr. Wyatt, "there's plenty of change here. A big increase in Theo's comprehension, his speech, clearly. His reading ability is ... incredible. His reflexes and muscle control. His physical strength. Seven-year-olds are bigger and stronger than four-year-olds. This is clearly the case for Theo. You've been diligent with his physical therapy. He's accelerating in every category we tested for."

The doctor they'd known for more than six years now, turned and grinned at them. "Theo has improved, *physiologically*."

Tears streamed down Carly's face freely. Jonathan sat ramrod straight in his chair, his hands firmly planted on his thighs for support. The shaking he felt throughout his body wasn't visible from the outside. He was quaking.

Jonathan saw that Theo would keep going, keep progressing and his life would hold endless progress, just like everyone else's life. And he could still see too that Theo wasn't doing what typical seven-year-olds were doing. He wasn't playing Little League, or making animations, or racing around the park with friends on razor scooters. But suddenly the whole point had changed. Effort, and progress, and self-satisfaction was what mattered. It was all that mattered. Theo would try, Theo would meet his own goals, and he'd be happy. He'd been happy all along.

—

When Jonathan and Carly were spit out onto the sidewalk in front of the doctor's office, they looked at each other, dazed.

"I'm craving diner food. Wanna go get some matzo ball soup and French fries?" Carly asked.

"Yes, I do."

They walked into The Flame Diner on the corner of 58th Street and 9th Avenue and both slid in on opposite sides of a booth. Carly pushed her large satchel purse into the corner and drummed the table with her fingertips.

"I don't even have to look at the menu."

Jonathan noticed that she didn't place her phone on the tabletop, off to the side, as Sara always did, as almost everyone does, turning a restaurant table into a personal desk, turning a shared meal into a diversion while awaiting messages. Carly was never the type to stay connected to her phone. In fact, when they'd met, she didn't even have one.

"Well, don't judge." Jonathan said, opening a menu.

They both ordered and sat for a moment in silence.

"We went to that diner after every birthing class. The one on Atlantic."

"Yeah. Maybe being in a hospital with you made me think of it."

Jonathan smiled weakly.

Their food arrived.

"I seem to keep pissing off Aimee."

Carly raised just her eyes from her spoonful of soup. "Oh, yeah? How and why?"

"I wish I didn't, it's not on purpose. She seems to think I fall short all the time with Theo and maybe that I'm an obstacle to her. We got along best while she was in Ireland.

"Hmm. Could be. She's like Maria."

Jonathan raised his eyebrows. "Who?"

"*The Sound of Music.* You're dense and self-important and don't see your own child and she's spirited and free. "Do Re Me Fa So La Ti Do."

"At least I'm against the Nazis. I'll have to rewatch that."

"You should try to get along with her. Theo adores her. She's helping Theo a lot. And she's far from home."

"She strikes me as rather rootless."

"That could be. You seem sad. Are you okay?" Carly spoke gently in a voice that made Jonathan feel vulnerable.

"I'm fine." Her assessing him openly was hard to run from. She had a way of looking and listening that was deeper than other people's. "I had a break-up last week. An abrupt dumping that was kind of rough." Jonathan coughed and looked away, horrified to say this to Carly.

Carly looked out the window. "I'm really sorry. That sucks."

"Thanks. It's no big deal. I'm better off actually."

"Hmm." Carly dipped a French fry in ketchup and ate it, immediately having another and another.

"What? I'm fine."

"Did you care about her?"

Was this a trick question? Not knowing the right answer, Jonathan went for the truth. "Yes, I did."

Anger flushed Carly's cheeks in a way Jonathan knew too well. "Then how about you be upset for a minute? Carly looked around the table and grabbed the ketchup, forcefully squirting more on her plate.

"I'm sad. You saw it yourself. It's just that I'm going to be okay. I can handle it."

"How about you not be *okay*? How about you let yourself be hurt, and fucked up, and unable to handle things. Wouldn't that be a good exercise for you? How about you be a little heart-broken for five minutes?"

"This is a weird conversation to be having with my ex-wife. You're desperate for me to be heartbroken over another woman."

"Well, I never got to see you heartbroken over me, or over Theo." Carly's mouth opened in the upside-down way that babies bawl, silent and with eyes closed. She began to weep in the diner.

Jonathan reached out and touched her hand. "Carly, is that what you believe? That I was never devastated over us?"

Carly clutched her napkin and wiped her eyes and mouth.

"I was devastated, and I had to structure everything in my life to handle it. I had to. I had Theo. And no you. I had to pull myself together."

Carly looked at him tentatively. "I cried every day for weeks. And whenever I spoke to you, you sounded fine. Strong. Dealing with everything I couldn't deal with."

"Carly, I'm sorry. That's how I operate in a crisis. I cried too."

Carly dried her face with her napkin. "I hate these evaluations." She laughed with some effort.

Jonathan smiled even as his eyes teared up too. She had been his wife, but she'd become a stranger in his mind, who he didn't understand, because she'd shocked him with her departure.

"They certainly do a number on us."

On the sidewalk in front of the diner, they stood in the cold sunlight. Their conversation returned to afternoon logistics for Theo. Finally, they said goodbye. Their parting brought Jonathan relief; he was drained from their prolonged encounter. As he turned the corner to head to the subway, he stopped for a moment and thought of his argument with Aimee and now this unearthing with Carly, both a week after his relationship with Sara was rent to pieces. He was very far from being a person who believed in astrology. But this confrontational and destructive energy all around him, this conflict-rife time, made him briefly wonder if there was something in his stars to look out for.

Theo

MEE-MEE searching in our closets.

"There must be something here you can use." Her eyes half shut. She think.

I swim behind her and look too.

"Poles?"

Dada's ski poles. He carry them from winter cabin where I watch movies with my cousins.

Mee-Mee's eyes all open now.

"You want to try to stand with these? You understand?"

"I try."

"Theo. This is grand. I'm gonna hold you up, around the waist. I won't let you fall. And you lean on these poles too."

She pull me up. Hug me. She behind me, holding me from sinking. She make invisible hard spots for me to stand on.

"Lean on the poles and bend your knees. You're just going to stand–no walking. Just stand upright and don't fall over." Aimee let go.

"Don't sink." I correct her.

"Yes, don't sink. If you can do it for a whole minute, you get a sticker. Does Theo want a sticker?"

"Yes." I say. Legs shaking. "Heart sticker." My bare feet grip the hard spots, try to hold them and not let them slide away.

"It's just you. I'm not holding." Aimee's empty hands rise in the air.

I stand, like a surfer, riding the hard spots above the water. I watch my feet and count to ten. And then they slide away and it's just water. I sink but Aimee's arms are there before I go all the way down.

"Ten seconds, Theo. That's amazing."

12.

A IMEE MANEUVERED past Union Square with Theo, heading northeast. She kept catching glimpses of the Flatiron Building. It appeared and then ghosted her between other buildings and each glimpse gave her a fuller picture of the whole.

"Well look at that, Theo. It's actually a triangle." Finally, she could see it unfettered in its entirety. "Brilliant. I never thought a building was a work of art before."

Head towards the Flatiron from Union Square. Jonathan had said.

The Flat what?

You don't know the Flatiron Building? You're in for a treat. After the Chrysler, it's my favorite building. Not only an ingenuity of construction, but perfectly appointed in her corner of downtown New York. Not every building finds the perfect berth.

Aimee felt a shiver of elation move through her spirit. She'd had this sensation on and off lately, a rising tide of euphoria that ebbed into a thoughtless contentment. But at other moments she felt like a twisted rag, ready to cry. The Flatiron resembled an elegant dinosaur, or a tall and narrow ship. She had to agree with Jonathan here. She felt suddenly that she knew her own esthetic, and it was this. There was a taste of Dublin in its contours to her, and yet it was utterly New York. Old World was the phrase that came to her mind. She drank in the sight, enamored for one moment, and fatigued by the beauty and difficulties of New York the next.

She hadn't given much thought to Jonathan's work, and she suddenly wondered for the first time if he was important in the world of architecture. He was the boss, she was quite sure of that. He'd said Project Manager. He carried a square case of drawings, she presumed. She'd heard him on the phone once, with the Department of Buildings, and it was clear he knew his stuff and was an authority. She'd bet he was the type that often showed-up his boss, just by knowing everything. She couldn't really picture that Jonathan had a boss. She felt a small irritation acknowledging that he was *her* boss; but she managed to keep an upper hand. She was interested to see Jonathan's new building though, with the silly name, the Jetson. He wasn't the architect, so she wouldn't judge him on its overall design or beauty, but she wondered nonetheless if it would be beautiful. Naturally, it wouldn't resemble the Flatiron, her new penultimate, which was–she wasn't even sure–classical– art deco? The Jetson was probably solid glass as was the style in New York these days, and not to her liking.

"Come on, Theo. Let's go see your father's building."

The Jetson was at 21st Street between 5th Avenue and Broadway, and Aimee tried to approach it with a good view, to see it in its whole before she was beneath it. But her attention was fractured by maneuvering the sidewalk with Theo in the new electric wheelchair. She chose to walk by Theo's left side, the same way she always led a cow and mounted a horse.

"Good steering Theo. Not too fast, not too slow. It's fun this way, right?"

Theo chose not to respond, but his smile, with his two new adult front teeth showing gave Aimee her answer.

At a red light, kitty-corner from the Jetson, Aimee got a break from her vigilance with Theo in the wheelchair, to observe that the graceful building across from them was in fact the Jetson. It almost looked like a smaller sandstone Empire State Building. For the second time that day, Aimee wished she knew the names of styles of architecture. Was this art deco? It had some simple rectangular patterns rising up its thin sides. It appeared to be made of plain concrete, or wet sand; Aimee didn't know what materials a building could be made of she realized. The doors on the two sides she could see were a yellow metal that matched beautifully with the tan rising walls around them. Jonathan had built this, she thought with vicarious pride. Did he always manage to work on buildings he would like? She intuited, while looking up at it, waiting for the light to change, thinking briefly of his apartment, his clothing even, that Jonathan had made his mark on the appearance of the Jetson, and that he would be proud of this project.

Aimee squatted in front of the left wheel of Theo's chair. When she saw she had eye-contact and Theo's attention, she raised one arm and pointed up at the building before them.

"That's your Dad's building. He made that. Do you like it?"

Theo nodded vigorously. "Hooray! Daddy wins!" His voice was breathy and high-pitched.

Aimee stroked Theo's arm that lay on the armrest, fingers on the joystick. "It's a grand building. Let's go see your Daddy."

"Go!" Theo raised his arms like wings, ready to take off and fly across the street.

—

Jonathan had been waiting since lunch for Theo and Aimee to arrive. He glanced up the block-long lobby again and again.

Jonathan thought about Theo's recent progress while he packed up his drawings and put away the smaller tools in his podium workstation.

Standing still in the lobby of the nearly completed Jetson, Jonathan looked toward the eastern side of the building and remembered the single step his foreman had installed by mistake, that had been removed by jackhammer the following week, no more elegant method to remove a concrete foundation that was never supposed to be.

For the second time that day, Mr. Buckner, the guilty party in that error, passed him by. Once again, it was on the tip of Jonathan's tongue to say, "My son is coming in to visit.". There was no one at the Jetson who knew he had a seven-year-old son with special needs. Who knew anything about his personal life.

Buckner was halfway across the lobby, when Jonathan called out, "Stick around Buckner, if you have the time. My son is about to arrive. I'd like for you to meet him."

The foreman turned and stared. "Well, alright." He slowly walked back to where Jonathan stood. "Didn't know you were a family man."

"I have one son. Seven years-old."

"I have three daughters, eleven, nine, and five. Keeping me busy and broke."

So this is how people begin to share, thought Jonathan. Jonathan knew that he was viewed as a taciturn boss, and that this small foray into personal territory was noticeable to Buckner.

He saw Theo glide into the lobby, Aimee having pushed the large silver wheelchair access button on the outside of the building to make the automatic doors swing open, to the side of the revolving doors. Theo spotted him and with his right hand securely attached to the joystick, steering him forward, he waved with his free left hand. Aimee strode a few steps behind.

Theo glided across the lobby of this new skyscraper that he'd built, that he'd engineered, steering EZ as they'd come to affectionately call it, his eyes taking in the whole space.

"Here he is—Theo." Jonathan said with pride.

"Oh." Buckner may have said more, but Jonathan was walking toward Theo and Aimee already.

He squatted in front of his boy "Hi, Boomer. It's nice to see you here at my job. I'll show you everything. Want to meet some people I work with?"

Theo looked to Buckner.

"Frank, this is my son, Theo, and his nanny, Aimee."

"A pleasure to meet you both. Young man," he held his hand out to Theo. Theo shook hands as though he had shaken hands a hundred times before. Buckner shook Aimee's hand with equanimity as well. Maybe he wasn't callous as Jonathan had always thought. They were just unknown to each other. Which Jonathan was beginning to think was because of himself.

"Thanks for sticking around. Bring your girls through too anytime you want. This building is one to be proud of." Jonathan and Frank shook hands as well, as though to seal their successful work on the Jetson.

Theo was already peering around their bodies, down the long gleaming and empty marble-floored lobby. The line from an old song came to Jonathan's mind, "I've got a brand-new pair of roller skates ..." He imagined Theo was ready to glide at top speed.

"Alright, let's go!"

"Let's go!" Theo echoed, already on the move.

Jonathan followed, with an unfamiliar lightness in his chest. What had he been so worried about? *I'm done letting able-bodied be the unspoken norm.*

The following day, Carly called Jonathan in the early afternoon. She was breathless.

"Jonathan, we're at PT. Theo's therapist received the evaluation from Dr. Wyatt. He's brought in a walker. He wants Theo to try using a walker." Carly tripped over her own words they were coming so fast. "Jonathan, I'm so sorry you weren't here, but he stood on his own feet! He stood for almost a whole minute, holding the walker." Carly stopped and breathed heavily. "Oh my god. It's hitting me more from telling you." Her breathing grew heavier with crying. "Are you mad you're not here?"

"Carly." Jonathan stepped outside from the Jetson. He'd left his jacket and it was very cold. His teeth began to chatter, from cold or from nervous energy. "No, I'm not mad. Oh, Theo." Jonathan started to bawl as he clutched the phone to his ear, his arms wrapped around himself, in just a shirt in the cold winter air. "Our baby. You saw him? He stood by himself?"

Now Carly laughed. "Yes. He really did."

"Maybe I can come now." Jonathan looked up at the sun. He was outside the building already, he could just walk away. His son had stood on his own two feet. Theo stood.

"Well, sure. But we're ending the session right now. But, Jonathan. He's bringing the walker home. And Aimee isn't feeling well. So, I'll bring Theo to your place and wait for you to get home."

"Did Aimee see Theo standing too?" Jonathan walked back into the building. He would wrap up his day early and meet Carly and Theo at home.

"She did. She's very proud of him. She looked so ... satisfied. Anyway, I'll see you at your place when you get home."

When Jonathan arrived home he heard music from the hallway before opening his front door. It was Nina Simone singing, I Wish I Knew How It Would Feel to Be Free. A Carly favorite. Through the door and very walls, the music rang out triumphantly. The song conveyed determination, hope and glory.

When he opened the door and came inside his own home, his arrival went unnoticed. Carly was in the open kitchen area— out of sight except her outstretched arms, her hands gesturing, *come, come.*

Theo was standing in the living room, his back turned to Jonathan. His wiry arms trembled as he gripped the handles of his new walker.

In the quiet between two songs, he heard sounds that seemed like an accompaniment to the music, a light thump as Theo struck out at the floor with the front wheels and the rubberized back feet of the walker, and then two swishes, his left foot sliding forward, leaving his hips rotated, and then his right catching up, straightening him out again, getting him one step closer to his destination. Three jerky movements, a three-step percussive rhythm without ceasing, thump, swish, swish. Theo didn't pause between steps. He'd waited a long time for this.

Jonathan wasn't envious that he wasn't the one Theo walked to. It was profound, and perhaps all he could handle, to watch from across the room, to witness. And once again, Jonathan was learning something new from Carly. He would be sidestepping right next to the walker, step for step, pacing Theo. Ready to catch him or assist him. Jonathan knew for sure that Aimee would also know to let Theo do it alone.

The fact that Theo's eyes were flashing with fierce effort, his mouth open in concentration, his breath audible too, let Jonathan know that walking to your goal—the person whose admiration you seek, and not having that beloved admirer shadow your every move, was what Theo needed. Theo had waited patiently for over five years for his legs to carry him again.

Theo was shaking all over by the time he reached the kitchen threshold. When he raised his front wheels on the wood door-jamb between the living room and kitchen tiles, he robotically stepped forward with his left foot before lowering the back legs on the walker, all his muscles gave out at once as his balance was thrown and he fell over, forwards and sideways, within the red cage of the walker. He knew no methods to break his fall and fell like a short tree.

Jonathan cried out but went unheard over the loud music. While his heart lurched into his throat and his blood rose to his scalp, Carly came into sight and lifted Theo out of the tangle and hugged him. Theo whimpered and put his head in Carly's lap.

"Look what you did! Do you know what you did, Theo? You walked across this whole room! You walked all by your-self." Theo stopped whimpering, listening to his mom's praise. "When a runner wins a long race, what do they do? They fall down on the ground and they yell, I did it!"

Jonathan thought that Carly hadn't noticed him until she added, "And Daddy saw the whole thing. He's so proud of you too."

Theo looked toward the front door at Jonathan. Jonathan remembered the forty nights, or so, that he walked through this same door at night and Theo had run to him. Before the illness. And this new memory of Theo grasping with all he had for his feet to carry him, was as cherished as those long ago, gone days.

Jonathan stumbled to his child. To Theo.

13.

AIMEE AWOKE again with the violent dream fresh in her head. This time she had been punching herself in the face, over and over again. The dream was fragmented. She was wearing something strange, a lacey white frock, a nightgown that she shouldn't have been wearing. Then she stood alone in a church and punched her face.

Every morning since December 31st, her waking thought had been, *why did I have sex with Connor? Why did I do that to another woman?* If only regret could erase the thing one regretted. She was tired rather than refreshed as she got out of bed to shower and get ready. She had class and then Theo at 3:00.

She wore the same jeans and same large sweater she'd been wearing through January and February. She was sick of winter. While she tried to tame her hair, wilder than ever, into a style other than a ponytail, *couldn't it lay flat for once,* she thought for the first time, maybe I'm depressed. This was the saddest she could remember feeling. The thoughts of Connor and yelling at her dad persisted through her days. But even when she wasn't thinking of her horribly tainted trip home, she felt slow-witted and sad. She needed spring to arrive, she decided.

She thought of Theo, and how new it was to navigate the world with him as he used the wheelchair. This should lift her up, but even thoughts of Theo were not enough to break her foul mood. She decided she would take Theo out for cookies and hot chocolate from the school bus. They'd go to that large café on Smith Street, where the wheelchair easily passed between tables. Aimee resolved to find her spirit and strength again. As she'd eased her conscience dozens of times this terrible winter, she pretended to know that Connor and Margaret had gone on a honeymoon somewhere in Europe, had moved joyfully into their marriage, and that he had not looked back even once to their crime. She should do the same.

—

Aimee waited on Jonathan's stoop for the school bus to arrive. It was March 1st and still winter. The lecture she'd attended earlier that day had been on statistics, which Aimee knew little to nothing about and found less than riveting. She'd gone out for Banh Mi after class with two friends from school. She'd genuinely laughed out loud when one friend described her roommate's hygiene rituals and obsessive-compulsive tooth-brushing habits. But she felt low and sluggish again. She thought of her cows. They were complacent and content, preferred things exactly the same day after day. Harmless creatures, better than she could say for humans, but she wasn't used to feeling like a cow, wanting nothing more than a clean bed and to rest.

The bus pulled up. Aimee greeted the driver, Mr. Yang by name, and she assisted Theo getting off, while Mr. Yang carried down the folded electric wheelchair. Aimee said hello to the three other kids on the bus, who were yet to be dropped at their front doors. These kids spent two to three hours a day on a school bus. Here or anywhere, they were not accustomed to strangers acknowledging them. Aimee liked to think she saw a spark of light in their eyes from her greetings. She always said hello to each of them, after giving Theo a hug and lifting him to carry him down the narrow front steps of the bus, her one exception about not carrying him.

Finally, Theo was settled in the chair, coat and hat on, backpack attached to the chair's handles and the bus was gone.

"We're off. Would you like a hot chocolate?"

"I do!" Theo pushed the joystick forward and Aimee hustled to keep up as they moved at a clip down Smith Street.

Aimee scanned the room and saw a café table with enough clearance on the side to comfortably park the wheelchair between table and wall. She maneuvered into the area, taking over the control of the chair to squeeze between other customers.

"Theo, wait here, I'll go up and get our food."

"Black and white."

"What's black and white?" Aimee whispered, glancing around with her head down, hoping Theo wasn't talking about people in the café.

"My cookie."

Aimee laughed. "You're communicating just fine, aren't you?"

"Yes."

"Ha—one Black and White coming right up."

Aimee ordered herself a cappuccino, her usual, even though it didn't sound good in the moment. She had a passing thought that she wanted only ice water but got none.

They sat in silence while Theo ate his cookie with rapt attention and Aimee sipped her milky cappuccino in tiny sips. Her mouth was filling up with saliva, and she fearfully realized she was going to vomit.

Without saying anything to Theo, she ran to the bathroom, and didn't even have time to latch the stall before she puked into the toilet, barely leaning over, it came so fast. The vomit was so disgusting to her, it made her wretch again and again. When her body stopped quaking and the fruity smell was flushed away, she stood there breathing heavily.

"Shite! Shite! Shite! Shite!" It had been nine weeks since New Year's Eve. She'd had no period. She felt like a fecking exhausted cow. She was pregnant. Aimee looked down at her stomach pressing into her Levi's waistband. She was wide-eyed with horror. The words *unwanted pregnancy* floated by her. The words took on a whole new meaning. To be pregnant and to very much not want to be pregnant, was like being assaulted. Her thoughts ran to self-defense, to escape, to outrun this assailant, to fight. She was also bitterly angry. "No! No, no, no, no, no. You fecking idjit." She began to sob. She had to get back out there to Theo. Aimee violently wiped away tears.

At the sink, she splashed water on her face and cupped water in her hand and rinsed out her mouth multiple times. She looked in the mirror. "You idjit!" She remembered the dream where she punched herself in the face.

Had her sleeping self known?

Maybe she wasn't pregnant.

Across the street was a CVS drugstore.

Aimee strode out of the bathroom with one desperate hope, maybe she wasn't pregnant. She began praying. She looked at Theo quickly as she walked past to the exit. The barista was squatting in front of him, turning the pages of the book Theo had brought with them. Aimee raised her pointer finger to the two of them, gesturing, 'I'll be right back.'

She ran across Smith Street to the CVS. She found the pregnancy tests on the shelf in under a minute and ran to the registers. There were three people in line. Aimee peered around their backs impatiently. The barista had seen her, right? Theo's back had been turned. The first customer was taking forever. She was asking effing questions, talking on and on, good lord. Where were more cashiers?

Minutes ticked by and it was still the same customer being helped. The two people in front of Aimee appeared to be asleep, staring at their phones, they were that unconcerned with the wait. Aimee shifted repeatedly and sighed audibly minute after minute. She debated stealing the pregnancy tests. The next customer finally reached the counter. Damn, she had a basket on the floor that Aimee hadn't seen.

"Are there more cashiers somewhere?" Aimee yelled from the line.

"Pharmacy in back," the young woman said without looking up from her scanning of items.

Aimee ran to the back, glancing out the windows toward the café. *I'll be right back. I'm coming right back.*

Aimee paid for the pregnancy tests with shaking hands. The pharmacist placed the box in two plastic bags.

Aimee took it and stared, scared to the point of despondency. "Do you have a bathroom?"

The young pharmacist looked over her shoulder. She opened the white swinging door beside her. "Come in. You can use the employee one."

Aimee dashed in, "I'll be super-fast." She was speaking to Theo, who was just across the street. With the barista. *He knows I'll be right back.* It hadn't been ten minutes yet.

The instructions said to use with first morning pee. If it was negative, she'd re-test in the morning. She peed on the stick and placed it flat on her thighs and watched. "Hurry, hurry!" The results were instantaneous, like a nightmare metamorphosis of the tiny white screen. The screen immediately came alive with the reading of her urine, a light gray shadow moved from right to left, at the speed of a crawling spider, and two pink lines rose to the surface. No need to wait the ten minutes. There they were. Two lines meant pregnant. "Mummy," she whimpered. "Mum, what do I do?"

Aimee rocked herself, still seated on the toilet, her jeans around her feet. The pregnancy test, incriminating and sentencing her, pressed between her stomach and thighs as she bent over and cried. She pulled herself together for Theo.

Aimee sat upright and put the pregnancy test in the garbage canister on the wall and stood. She pulled up her pants and buttoned them, finally noticing that they were too tight. She left the stall. Then immediately turned around and went back in and fished the pregnancy test out of the garbage box. It was still there, still positive.

"Oh you poor, poor baby."

She shoved the test in her jacket pocket. She'd hesitated to spend $100 on this down Northface jacket. She'd been coveting it. Twenty-three, poor, unmarried and pregnant. *Why did she even leave Ireland for this fate?*

Aimee hustled out of the bathroom and scanned the small pharmacy area, to avoid getting the helpful young woman in trouble. No one was around and she ran out to the store, to the exit. Within seconds she was out on the sidewalk again, looking toward the large windows at the front of Café DuNord across the street.

"Theo!" She called out as she ran across the street mid-block. But she could already see through the café's large front window that Theo was no longer seated at their table.

She stumbled through the front door, and went all the way to their seats, as though maybe reaching it, touching the white marble with her palms would make Theo and his wheelchair reappear. Aimee ran to the counter. "Is the boy in the bathroom? The boy in the wheelchair? Where is he?"

The young woman behind the counter gave Aimee a dirty look. "Where were *you*? He was crying and alone. He wouldn't talk. Does he speak? The police just picked him up two minutes ago."

"Why did you let them take him?" Aimee demanded in a loud voice. She looked down and saw that her jacket had some vomit on it. Her shoes were splattered with vomit. "Where have they taken him?" She wailed.

"I don't know. I called 911, they came and they took him. Call 911, I guess."

Aimee rushed away from the counter and tore open the front of her backpack to find her phone, to call 911. The entire café was staring at her. An older woman *tsked* her tongue and shook her head. "And to think, she's in charge of that handicapped boy."

Did she really say that?

The operator answered and Aimee spoke so frantically that her accent magnified. "I'm lookin fahr a little boy, who de pahlice pecked oehp. He's seven, 'is name is Theo.

"Ma'am, please repeat."

Aimee took a deep breath and tried to utilize the American accent she'd developed. "Please, can you help me? The police have picked up the boy I babysit, from Café DuNord in Carroll

Gardens. I need to get him, can you tell me where they've taken him? He's disabled." Aimee couldn't hold back a sob.

"What's your location?"

"I've lost a child!"

"I heard you, Ma'am. What's your location?"

After an excruciating five minutes of questions and answers, Aimee was given the number for the local precinct. She called and was told that Theo was there. It was five blocks away. Aimee ran the whole way.

As soon as Aimee introduced herself and said why she was there, the officer at the desk asked her to come in and stay with the "unidentified minor."

"Theo Brooks. That's his name. He is identified. Is he alright?"

But Aimee could already see Theo through an open doorway, in an inner room, and she was already pushing through the half door and running to Theo."

"Theo!"

Theo turned his head toward Aimee's voice and pivoted the wheelchair toward her. Headed her way. Aimee ran to Theo and wrapped her arms around his narrow shoulders.

"I'm so sorry, Theo! I went to the bathroom; I was sick. I'm so sorry I left you, Theo. Are you okay?"

"Mee-Mee not there. I'm alone." Theo whispered.

"I'm sorry." Aimee cried. "Please forgive me."

"I forgive you."

Aimee froze hearing the maturity in Theo's voice.

"Are you okay? Do you need to use the bathroom?"

"No." Theo stroked Aimee's cheek, "You're crying."

"I'll stop now. I got scared. I'm sorry."

"Excuse me," the officer interrupted. "We need a legal guardian to release the boy. Are you his guardian?" His voice sounded doubtful.

"I'm his baby-sitter."

"We need a name and phone number for a guardian. You'll need to stay until a parent or guardian arrives."

"Of course! I'm not going anywhere." Aimee heard the righteous indignation in her voice. Even though she had done just that—gone somewhere. Aimee moaned as she looked at the dry vomit on her jacket and imagined Jonathan arriving. Theo began to whimper, picking up on Aimee's anxiety.

Which parent's name would she give? Both choices were unbearable to contemplate.

Jonathan would rage and fume. He'd charge in and rescue Theo. Would he fire her? And she was pregnant. She'd forgotten for the past twenty minutes in her panic over Theo, and now the horrible fact had come back. This would happen again and again she realized, forgetting and then the crushing remembering.

And Carly. Carly would stonewall her. She'd comfort Theo and deal with the police calmly and efficiently. She'd ask Aimee questions, like a *Garda* herself. She'd get the full story and then she'd freeze Aimee out forever. Turn her irrelevant with her disdain.

In a tiny elevator in the back of a hotel in County Kerry, Aimee had sealed her fate. She and Connor had come together in a frenzy inside that small space, and they had set something in motion. Aimee would pay for that sin for the rest of her life, and now so had Theo.

Theo whimpered and whispered, "Go home now," in a tiny voice, while Aimee tried to decide who's name to offer up. Jonathan would rage and shout, but would possibly forgive her. Carly would remain calm and get them through the situation, out of the police station, and then would decimate Aimee, like a mother wolf to her rival– swift obliteration.

"Call his mom, Carly Brooks. I have her number right here."

—

Carly was setting up the art room at PS 9 Elementary School, on the second floor of the newly acquired space, organizing and tidying the supplies and arranging the cluster tables, when her phone rang. She hadn't had a chance to tell Jonathan that she was going back to work. She liked making life decisions without having to consult him. Actually, there were very few decisions she felt free to make without him, even after nearly four years of separation. Co-parenting prevented that freedom. She worried briefly that taking a full-time job was not a decision she was entitled to make alone, as she answered the call from an unknown number.

She listened. The room froze. Dust motes stilled in the air. There was utter silence. Her eyes moved to the clock on the wall, and she could hear her blood moving in her inner ears. It was important to see the time on that school clock, with a red seconds hand. It was 4:03 and then it was 4:04. The police had picked up Theo alone. There was now a Ms. O'Malley there with him at the police station. It was Carly's own speaking voice that unfroze the claustrophobic air around her and put oxygen back in her body.

"Thank you," were Carly's first words. Said not to the officer on the phone, but to the universe. She sucked in air. "Give me your address please and I'll be right there. Where are you located?" And then as a crucial after-thought, "Please put my son on the phone. Will you?"

A moment later, after hearing a shuffle and a breath and then loaded silence, Carly knew Theo held the phone receiver to his ear.

"Baby. Are you there? It's me, Mommy."

"Mommy." Theo said, with a tremor in his voice. "I'm Police Station. City of Brooklyn Police Department."

"Are you reading, honey?"

"NYPD. Pre … seen-seent 76."

"Thanks Sweetie. That's super helpful. The police picked you up in a café, right? Are you okay?"

"Do not enter be-yond this point."

"Okay, babe. Are you scared?"

"No scared. Mee-Mee now."

"You're safe, Sweetie. I'm coming for you." Carly felt a sob in her throat even though the danger was past.

There was a shuffling of skin, fabric, plastic and then Aimee's voice, "Hi," she sounded very young and very scared in the one small syllable. Over the phone, Aimee began sobbing, startling Carly out of her singular mindset.

"Carly … I'm so sorry. I had an emergency. I thought I was only gone for a few minutes, it was way too long. I left him." Aimee tried to catch her breath and stifle her sobs. "I'm sorry. I'm so sorry."

"Does he seem okay?"

"Yes."

"Okay, calm down. Try to calm down or you'll scare Theo. I'm coming right now." Carly was already down the hall of the school, clutching her cellphone to her ear, unsure if she had collected her belongings in the room, desperate to get to Theo and create normalcy and safety. She envisioned reading books to Theo on the couch before making dinner; her primal brain told her to get through all the inevitable bureaucratic and logistical steps ahead: a car service, showing her ID, police paperwork, dealing with Aimee, calling Jonathan, a car service again, the wheelchair, all the required steps that she'd execute to get to the safety and comfort of those picture books on the couch with Theo home safe.

—

When Carly breathlessly entered the police station and saw Theo and Aimee seated side-by-side, she knew instantly that she couldn't dismiss Aimee as she badly wanted to. At a glance, she saw something she'd never seen before. They were two youths. They were near-peers. Theo had some strengths that Aimee didn't. Aimee's strengths were externally obvious and superior to Theo's. But Theo had inner security that showed. For the first time, Carly noticed the instability at the heart of Aimee. And she guessed in that moment that the girl was motherless.

Aimee had said at Christmas that she was visiting her father in Ireland. *Was there no mother?* Theo was dry-eyed and calm. No signs of distress anymore. Aimee was the one with puffy, red eyes. She was disheveled and even looked dirty. *Were her clothes dirty? Had they ever been before?*

Theo didn't look so young anymore, in his sleek wheelchair, his newly acquired upright posture; and Aimee looked ridiculously young, like a teenager. *Through the looking glass. Two kids.*

Carly strode to Theo and embraced him. Holding Theo, she couldn't take her eyes off Aimee. Theo whooped with relief, "Whoo, whoo, Mommy!" He was fine. *He's safe.*

Aimee's head was tilted down. She did not meet Carly's gaze.

An hour later, Carly and Aimee sat at Carly's kitchen table. Theo played on the living room rug with trains and wooden tracks he'd learned to put together himself. It was already dark outside. Carly drank black tea. She'd put on the kettle as soon as they arrived. Aimee had accepted a cup of chamomile.

"So, what happened?"

Aimee looked resolute, finally calm. "I made a huge mistake and I'm really sorry. I know how serious it is to have left Theo alone in public. I know I'm fired. I'm so sorry. I'm going to go now."

She stood. "I can't say goodbye to Theo just now. I just can't." Aimee covered her mouth with her hand.

Carly rose. "But why did you leave him? What happened?"

"I'm going to throw-up!" Aimee ran for the bathroom.

When Aimee returned, Carly was still seated at the table. She'd put out a plate of tea biscuits.

With her eyes fixed on the plate of cookies, Aimee said, "I'm pregnant." She looked mortified and numb. Carly could feel the embarrassment radiating off her. Carly always saw Aimee's resolve, her absolute strength. Now something else was revealed. Carly had wanted to know what happened. And what happened was this news, this discovery. It is why she left Theo.

"Can I have one of those?" Aimee pointed, like Theo himself might, to the cookies.

Carly rose. "Sit down. I'll make you some toast."

Aimee sat and ate a cookie before speaking. Then she ate half of another in one bite. She chewed methodically.

"I suddenly felt sick at the café. I rushed to the bathroom and vomited. I realized I might be pregnant and I just panicked. I ran across the street, to get a test. The barista was with Theo, but I didn't ask her to watch him for me. If only I had asked her, none of this would have happened."

"They called 911. The police had just taken Theo when I came running back in." Aimee frowned, seeming to disapprove of her own words.

Carly brought over the toast, and a glass of cold water. She pulled her chair further out from the table so she could see Theo playing on the floor in the next room. She longed to go join him. She was conflicted with her sympathy for Aimee and a sense of obligation to help, and her desire for the comfort of just being with Theo. She felt she had to muster her anger. It had waned. She was depleted.

Carly spoke quietly. "I know you understand the gravity of what happened. That leaving Theo alone in a café is totally unacceptable. I know you're sorry. And I know that Theo is very dear to you too." Carly took a deep breath. "Another day soon, when we're both feeling calmer, we can talk about the responsibility you have to Theo. And if we can trust you with that much responsibility."

Aimee nodded. "Do you mind if I eat? I'm really hungry."

Carly opened one palm to Aimee, "It's for you." A horrible notion came to Carly–had someone taken advantage of this girl alone in New York?

"I'm sorry to ask you something so personal–was it a boyfriend, or lover, someone you chose to have sex with?"

Aimee looked up at Carly, seeming to read her meaning. "It was consensual. An old boyfriend in Ireland. I don't want a baby. I have no idea how to be a mother."

"Is your mother alive?"

Aimee's whole body twitched, the half-eaten piece of toast in her hand, her fingers shiny with butter. She shook her head. "My mum died when I was very little." Her tears spilled on her face.

Carly stood and moved around the table next to Aimee. She wrapped her arms around the girl. "Alright. It's okay Aimee. Let it out."

Theo

MEE-MEE LOOKED at me as she ran to the jacks. Her face was gray like a sky. Her mouth a straight line.

The café lady read to me and I waited.

When the book ended I started to worry. "Mee-Mee?"

"You want your Mommy?"

"No. Where Mee-Mee?"

Long time goes by. Police come. Again I say, "Where Mee-Mee?" I try not to cry, but can't hold it in. They wheel me to their car. I say, "No! Wait for Mee-Mee."

"It's okay little guy. We'll find your Mommy."

When Mee-Mee comes to police station she looks funny still, like her face was washed and everything moved a little bit around. She hugs me and she smells kind of bad. I don't care. Mee-Mee and I are together.

Mommy comes too. Now everything alright again.

14.

CARLY CALLED Jonathan late at night after finally saying goodbye to Aimee and getting Theo to bed. He'd already gone to bed and didn't pick up, so the following morning he listened to a cryptic message from Carly, "*Can you come by tomorrow morning to talk, its fairly urgent.*"

They had recently changed Theo's schedule to even out the number of nights they each had, and Jonathan was still getting used to Theo being away from him Sunday and Monday night. Listening to this message in the early morning, Jonathan was apprehensive.

It served as a reminder that recently he and Carly had been getting along better than they had since the separation. It had been some time since either of them had left stressful, urgent messages.

He texted Carly. "Are you and Theo okay? Wanna talk now?"

She responded almost instantly. "We're both okay. Sorry. I'm getting ready to take him to school. Would rather talk in person."

"How's 9?"

"Perfect. Thanks for not questioning me."

Jonathan stared at his phone. If they were fine, what was up? Could it be Carly wanted to move forward with their divorce? He inhaled and closed his eyes. He'd wait and find out.

As he gathered his wallet and keys to leave, he remembered the corner protectors he'd bought for Carly's apartment and he grabbed them from his broom closet. He left his building and decided he'd take a Citibike to Carly's apartment in Fort Greene. Jonathan swiped his bank card and released a bike from the station at the corner. Since he hadn't brought his helmet, he checked on his phone for the route that had bike lanes. It was a short ride, and with the wall panels tucked under his left arm, he rode one-handed, cautiously and without haste.

Jonathan hadn't ridden a bike in several years. Pedalling through Brooklyn in the cold morning air, he experienced an itch for change that was potentially thrilling, but also agitating. He felt ready for something new. He knew that people could create positive transformation or destruction under this urge. As he noticed the different stores and restaurants of Carly's neighborhood, he felt like a traveller in a new city. Jonathan liked being unfamiliar with his surroundings. He wondered if he might change his life. He had no plans, just an abrupt and uncertain desire for growth.

"Come in." Carly said, holding the door open for him. "I'll make coffee."

"I'm good. I've already had one."

"Okay. Well let's sit in the kitchen."

Jonathan followed her. He set the corner protectors beside the opening to the kitchen. A passageway that would receive one of them, the corner was chipped all the way down to the metal framing from Theo steering EZ into the door jambs.

"What are those?"

"Corner protectors. A little industrial looking, but there's no sense in re-plastering while he's still crashing into the walls repeatedly."

"How thoughtful. Thank you."

"Didn't I mention I'd bring you some? I guess I just thought it. I put them up at my place.

They sat down. Carly laughed nervously.

"I'm not sure where to begin."

"You're scaring me. Don't keep me guessing, Carly."

"Sorry. You don't need to be scared." But still Carly was stuck. Her eyes darted and Jonathan knew she was trying to figure out the best phrasing.

"The beginning. From the beginning should work."

"Yesterday Aimee left Theo in a café alone for about twenty minutes."

Jonathan had to sort that out, like a math equation, before it computed. Theo alone in public for twenty minutes.

"They went for a snack. Aimee felt sick. She had to rush to the bathroom and vomit. She came back out and saw that Theo was engaged with a staff from the café, by your place, they know Theo, sort of, anyway, Aimee ran across the street to a drug store.

She panicked.

She needed a pregnancy test. Because she threw up she thought she might be pregnant. She took the test at the pharmacy. She came back to the café and the police had picked up Theo because he was alone for too long." Carly took a breath.

It took his brain a fraction of a second to process what she said, and he felt a mini-explosion, almost like an aneurism with this understanding.

Jonathan had once driven a speedboat during a lightning storm in the Finger Lakes when he was in high school. He and two friends had gone on a fishing trip. A summer storm kicked up out of nowhere and the sky was zig-zagged with lightening like he'd never seen before, like a child's drawing. There were four different harbors on this ten-mile lake, and they were equal distance from each. There was no way of knowing which one to steer towards or if the lightening would be drawn to their boat or not. It was gloomy and scary and dramatic, and Jonathan never found out if it had been truly dangerous or not. Racing across that lake, amongst the flashes of lightning, came back to him vividly as he listened to Carly.

"Is Theo okay?"

"Yes. He handled it really well. I know I should have called you. But, I raced to the station to get to Theo. When we finally got home, I had to deal with Aimee. I was very firm about how serious this was. I just wanted to be with Theo, to physically hold him. Later, I was so exhausted from the stress that I fell asleep in his bed. I called you when I woke up."

"Is she pregnant?"

"Yes. There's that. The police called me. Aimee had already arrived at the station, but a parent was needed to release Theo. Aimee was devastated. She felt ... ashamed."

"I should hope so."

Carly paused and nodded. "She fucked up. But then she told me she's pregnant. And I noticed for the first time that she's not all together and strong as she might seem. Well, not now she isn't. She's very broken-up. That's why I told her to take the week off." Carly groaned and then laughed nervously.

"What in the world is funny?"

"I applied for my old job, at the school. I'm going to be the art teacher again. That seemed like big news, before."

"Full-time?"

"Yes. I think I'm ready. Don't you think we can make it work?"

"When we had Aimee, it would work. We'll make it work." They sat a moment in silence, each contemplating how their lives would work now without Aimee. "You did the right thing. She abandoned Theo." Jonathan uncrossed his legs and pressed the table, straight-armed. "We'll make it work. What does she want to do?"

"You mean the pregnancy? I don't know for sure. She said she doesn't want a baby. I tried to ask if she was raped."

"Jesus, Carly. Why did you think that?"

"It's fairly common. I don't know. I feared the worst. She looked so wrecked. It was one hour after learning she's pregnant."

"And one hour after leaving Theo."

"She was horrified that she'd abandoned him. She was really so sorry."

Jonathan stood. "Alright. Well, employers don't make these choices for their nannies. For a second I thought we had to figure this one out. I'll install the corners."

Carly stared at him. She sat tall on the edge of her chair. Jonathan was surprised to see tears running down her face.

"She abandoned our child, Carly. In a wheelchair in a café. She can't just walk off, leaving Theo, even in an emergency."

Carly swiped at fresh tears. "That's exactly what I'm thinking … about her. We can't just walk away from Aimee. You've always told me that a skyscraper is only as strong as its weakest point. One infinitesimal mistake and the whole thing will crash down. People are the opposite. We're as strong as our strongest points. We're not always at our most perfect, but it's in there and we should be known for that."

"It's her job to care for Theo. She failed."

"People look out for each other even when it's not their job. Who's taking care of Aimee?"

—

Jonathan and Aimee walked in Prospect Park. It was the end of her week off, and Jonathan had had plenty of time to think, but he had no idea what Aimee was thinking. It was extremely cold, too cold for a walk in the park, and therefore it seemed they had the whole Olmstead paradise to themselves.

"This is the first time we've spent time together without Theo." Jonathan said.

Aimee burrowed deeper into her down jacket, her hands swaddled in giant mittens. "When you invited me for a walk on a 20-degree day, I figured it wasn't to watch Theo. Walk the plank, more like it."

"We don't want you to walk the plank. But I'll be honest, you're not capable right now of watching Theo. You're in a crisis, is what I've been told. I rather leave Theo out of the picture."

Aimee's step faltered, and her mouth made an unhappy fold and remained slammed shut. Jonathan felt her emotional pain like a wave of heat coming from her.

"We're concerned, Aimee. Carly and I want to know how you are, where you're at." Jonathan took a breath. "This temperature is untenable, let's go find someplace to warm up and get a hot drink."

They headed out toward 15th Street, the closest exit from where they were. They walked in silence.

Jonathan didn't know how to get back to where they were before this all happened. What were the words that would return them to when Aimee was bossy, self-righteous, and always right? The Aimee who had crossed the Atlantic and opened doors in Theo's brain. Jonathan recalled their first meeting, not for the first time, how Aimee had peered into Theo's face for a long moment, with an almost scolding expression that said, "What are you doing, child? Have you had enough of this game yet?"

And Theo's face when Aimee was in the room. More lights on behind his eyes. He woke up. Jonathan saw the flame of curiosity turn on, and he recognized it from his own awakenings after periods of boredom, or un-nameable sadness. He saw himself in Theo's upswing.

He couldn't roll back time to before Aimee had left Theo alone in the café. He couldn't pull forth the young woman who had been all strength in their lives, who he had leaned on for half a year as a partner with Theo.

He couldn't bring back the very best day he'd spent with Sara either. A time they hiked at Bear Mountain and they lost the trail. It seemed impossible to end up in danger at Bear Mountain, but it grew dark as they'd talked for hours with so much laughter and openness. They drank the last of their water and they made love in a tight gathering of trees. The trees complicit in their romance, hiding them from sight. When they rose from the pine needles it was dark and there were stars like Christmas balls of light above. It had been a warmer season then. They walked out to the road that had seemed to lead to nowhere and a ranger drove by. He drove them the six miles to Jonathan's car, Sara's hand tucked in his. That day was gone forever, folded into the continuum of time.

More poignantly yet, he could not bring back the true, grand love of his life, his years with Carly. He'd designed the diamond ring he proposed to her with. It was an emerald cut diamond, with baguettes along the sides and it was raised upon an air-filled empty space, as were the baguettes, it was like a squat Eiffel Tower. The jeweler he'd collaborated with showed him the final product with admiration. "I didn't know what you were doing with this design, but as I forged the metal I finally saw what you were thinking. It's an architect's ring, that's for sure."

He'd had a plan to propose over dinner in their favorite restaurant for special occasions in Red Hook. But Carly came home and said she'd had a hard day and just wanted to order in and watch Mad Men. On a whim, Jonathan said, "Let's dress up." Carly wrapped her arms around him and didn't question the idea. "It's Friday night, why not?" She'd said.

She put on a dark brown satin dress with beaded straps and brown high heels, Jonathan put on a suit and shoes. Then they were laughing and feeling silly as Thai food arrived and they paid the delivery guy in their finery. Before they ate, Jonathan said, "You look so beautiful, let's have a dance." He put on, Louis Armstrong, *A Kiss to Hang a Dream On*, and he took Carly in his arms on the rug in their living room, in the home they'd already shared for three years, the home he lived in still with Theo. Neither of them knew how to slow dance with skill, but they always could do it well together. Their bodies touched at all the right places and moved together easily. She rested her head on his chest, laughing for real now at their antics. Jonathan pulled back his head and shoulders to make eye-contact, he hadn't planned the words to say, and what came out was, "Carly, will you marry me and try to have a baby with me?"

They'd hardly ever spoken of it, but it was a known fact between them that Theo was conceived that night. They'd made love, and three weeks later Carly had a positive pregnancy test.

Jonathan couldn't get that night or that marriage back intact either. The fourth dimension granted no wishes and repaired no mistakes. It swelled in only one direction, forever forward, a wave always tarrying toward the distant shore.

They sat at a table in a café neither of them knew. Aimee ordered a large mint tea and a scone. He drank black coffee.

Aimee surprised him by speaking first. "If I'm not fired, I need to quit. I've got a lot to work out right now."

Jonathan sipped his coffee. What did he want from her? Was this goodbye?

"Aimee, what's the hardest thing that ever happened to you in your life so far? Before this."

Aimee looked startled but didn't need time to think about it. "My mum. My mum dying. Finding my mum on the couch. And being alone with my mum too. She was an alcoholic. She got bolloxed every day, and I always felt like I was alone with her. Like, *'where is everybody else?'*"

Jonathan fiddled with his paper cup. "That sounds awful, and for a child." Many times in his life it had taken him months, even years, to have a personal conversation with someone. And when these intimate interactions happened, he always wondered, is this what other people do early on?

"I'm sorry, Aimee. And what's the best thing that ever happened to you?"

Aimee had to think on this one. Slowly, a proud expression crept into her face.

"I was ten, three years after my mum died. It was a sow. She was laboring. My dad had his arm all the way inside her and he felt the calf's back, it's spine. It was facing away from the birth canal. It had to turn around and get its forelegs towards the exit. That's all that was needed. It would slide out if its legs were facing the exit but it wasn't doing that and it was going to die in there, curled up like a ball. And it was gonna kill the sow right along with it if it didn't budge soon. But I was small enough to put both my arms inside her at one time. I had to hold my breath and press the side of my face on her vulva, to reach in there deep enough to use both hands and turn the torso of that calf. I almost had to put my head in that poor cow. But I did it. It was like grasping another kid, like pin-the-tail-on-the-donkey, the way we'd blindfold each other and then spin each other around. I turned that calf and her legs followed her body and then I grabbed her front hooves and slowly pulled her to me, right out of her mama. The other one practically spilled out just following her twin. Turned out they were twins, facing each other. I saved the cow and the two calves."

Jonathan burst out laughing. "That could be the *worst* thing that ever happened to me." No, seriously, that's wonderful." He leaned back in his chair. "You're going to be all right, Aimee. You're whole life is ahead of you, to plan as you will. In another year, you'll have a Master's degree."

Aimee sniffled and wiped her nose with her hand. "Actually, in three years I'll be a doctor." She looked down at her stomach and touched it with her fingertips. Her hand looked as young as she was. A girl's hand.

"Have you decided what to do?"

"If I have this baby, I can never go back to Ireland."

"Why?"

"I just couldn't." Aimee finally looked up at Jonathan. It seemed that he hadn't seen her eyes yet this entire day. She looked unhinged. "Actually, I think I was wrong. The worst thing that ever happened to me was what I did getting pregnant with this baby. And the best thing that ever happened to me is working with Theo."

"Theo is the best thing that ever happened to me. But there have been times when I thought the opposite. You know you helped me see that miscalculation."

Jonathan sketched on a napkin. He found he was drawing the same skyscraper he'd drawn since he was a kid. The Empire State Building, the Chrysler, the Eiffel Tower—elements of each—it's apex a chiseled narrowing point of infinite angles.

"If a skyscraper were a single plane, a tall upright face, the wind would blow it away. At their most vulnerable points, they require a series of faces, breaking up the impact of a 200 MPH wind. Curves, rotations in the façade, vents, broken lines in their structure in order to confuse the wind. It's the lack of singularity that makes a skyscraper strong, that makes it able to withstand the blows."

Jonathan looked out the large window beside them and the terrifically cold winter day. He waited to see something blown by the wind. Trash or a tree branch, the movement was always there. Turning back to the napkin, he drew waving lines coming toward his skyscraper.

"People too, are not one thing. I'm not just the ignorant dad who felt betrayed by Theo's differences. You're not just the young woman who's messing up her life right now."

—

Jonathan went to see Carly later that night, to tell her what he knew about Aimee, which was almost nothing. They already knew what they needed to know, which was that they needed a new nanny right away. In a way, Aimee's personal crisis made this decision easier. She didn't need to be fired for leaving Theo. She wasn't in a state where she could care for Theo. The three of them understood that.

His thoughts wound him up while he walked from the Dekalb train station to Carly's place. He didn't really need to see Carly, he needed to contact a nanny agency and work this out. He needed to find a special-needs babysitter.

Carly opened her front door with a question on her face.

"Hi. Is Theo still up?" Jonathan asked, suddenly wanting to hold his son.

"Just went to sleep."

Jonathan placed his heavy briefcase by the door and dropped into an armchair. "We need a new sitter. That's all I can tell you. It was very moving to talk with her. I should have been talking with her more all along. I have no idea what she's going to do. We did at least discuss that she can't care for Theo."

Jonathan abruptly felt exhausted. He wanted to lay down right there and take a nap. He felt certain it would be a solid, dreamless rest. He leaned his head back and shut his eyes and focused on his breathing. A minute later he felt a warm blanket laid across his knees.

"It's so cold outside. Sleep here tonight. I'll make up the couch."

"I just want to close my eyes a few minutes." But Jonathan awoke hours later in the dark. He looked to the couch where Carly had left pillows, sheets and a down comforter. He smiled knowing that Carly and Theo slumbered in the next room.

15.

AIMEE ENTERED Bellevue Hospital through the emergency room entrance. She walked straight to the bank of elevators and rode up to the 3rd floor Women's Medical Center. They had given her specific instructions for the quickest route to the clinic. There'd been no protesters to walk past, no eyes on her, as Aimee entered the women's clinic, signed in, and found a chair in the corner. She kept her coat and hat on while she sat there. With her hat pulled down over her eyebrows and her chin tucked in, she imagined no one could see her. Aimee stole looks at the women in the room around her. Were any of them here for an abortion? Were all of them? They could be here for pap smears, or birth control, or STD symptoms. Their faces were masks of privacy–just like hers. Nothing showed, pregnancies possibly hidden in still-flat stomachs, covered by winter coats and baggy clothes.

Aimee thought of the elevator in Castlemaine. She could still see the red stop button and Connor's index finger pressing it. She felt the abrupt jolt of the elevator stopping between floors. Suspended. They'd fucked, and one sperm had penetrated her egg which just happened to be making its migration at the same time. This thing—this organism had been set in motion before they'd even released the stop button and exited that tiny dumbwaiter. And it was well established by the time she left Ireland, two days later. Her body had worked exactly as it was designed to. If only it hadn't worked so well. Aimee didn't picture the embryo as a baby curled inside her. It was a mass of cells that firmly labelled Connor as a cheater and her as a gender-traitor. She'd sabotaged herself too. Add that to the list. She'd behaved as would be expected of Pauline's daughter. But she'd travelled so far from County Kerry and the girl who an alcoholic mum had birthed so late in life. She'd always been an unexpected success. Strong, smart, a striver, a girl who left home for bigger things.

But what of Pauline? Aimee didn't know what her mother thought about having *her*. What did she think of Aimee's appearance in her own womb at the age of forty-four? Of her arrival into their family, into Pauline's kitchen and Pauline's sewing room, and in front of the TV beside her each night, her gin glass in reach.

Aimee was seven when her mother died, and she had no real idea what her mother's feelings had been about her. She remembered the clothing her mother made for her. Apron fronted dresses with fabric belts that tied behind her back, dungarees with flannel lined cuffs, purely for decoration, a red knit poncho that Aimee loved to wear through one fall in particular, pretending she was Little Red Riding-hood, running through the trees on the farm. Pauline had told her how fun it was to make these clothes. "I 've bought all your brothers' clothes all these years. Didn't even know I had an urge to make clothes for my child until you came along." When Aimee seemed ready to walk, but wouldn't let go of her mother's finger, Pauline got on the floor and crawled two feet away, then three, then four, each time saying, "Come, baby girl," arms outstretched.

"O'Malley." A nurse with a file in her hand, called from the doorway to the inner rooms. Aimee stared. Why in the world were they calling her mother here? *Oh, me.* Aimee stood and walked through the doorway.

Aimee followed the nurse into an exam room. "You can hang your coat here on the door and put your belongings on the chair. How are you, today?"

Aimee reluctantly removed her coat and hat and put them on the arm chair by the window, the blinds were down and closed.

"Please have a seat." The nurse gestured to the exam table. "I just want to make sure you're aware of your options. It's required that I explain your options to you today. Sorry if you've already heard this. In addition to the availability of a safe and legal abortion today, you also have the right to keep your baby, or to carry the pregnancy to term and put the baby up for adoption. Would you like to discuss any of these options?"

"I'm here for an abortion."

The nurse nodded. "The procedure is safe and fast and the recovery is minimal. You'll go home and take the rest of the day easy, bed or couch, resting, television, walking around at home is fine. You'll need sanitary napkins for several days and will have bleeding and cramping. The cramping can be severe, with a heavy flow. But if you're in extreme pain or if the bleeding is excessive, call us immediately or go to the emergency room if we're closed."

"Okay. I won't need emergency care."

The nurse paused and smiled at Aimee. "No, I don't suspect you will. After tomorrow you can go back to all normal activities. But no intercourse for six weeks."

The thought of sex came as a shock to Aimee. The nurse handed her two hospital gowns. "Put on both of them, the first one open to the front, second open to the back. The doctor will be in shortly to do the procedure. Any questions?"

Aimee shook her head and held the gowns to her chest. The nurse reminded her slightly of Carly. They didn't look alike, but she was maternal and warm, and Aimee wouldn't have minded if the woman offered a hug, but she left the room.

Aimee got up on the table and unlaced her shoes, and removed them, hesitating and then leaving on her socks. She pulled off her jeans and underwear together and dropped them on the chair. Then she picked them up again and rolled them up, hiding the underwear inside the jeans. She remembered her underwear that night in the hotel and how Connor had gone to shove them in his pocket and she'd yelped, "Don't!"

She removed her sweater, but left her bra on. Aimee put on the first gown and tied the tiny string in the front, then put the second gown on in the opposite direction, unable to tie it herself in the back. She hoisted herself onto the table and sat upright there for a moment. Then she jumped down and went to the blinds, she turned the long plastic wand until the Levelors opened horizontally. She could see the street and the herd of cars moving uptown below on 2nd Avenue.

Pauline had narrated so many things to Aimee. As a baby, she'd held her up against windows in the winter and said, "Look, snow. And there's Daddy pulling the tractor into the barn. Daddy, the farmer." She'd laughed. The board books they perused over and over were full of farm animals, farmers and tractors. But Aimee had the real thing all around her.

As Aimee grew older, Pauline's narration had matured along with her. They drove to town daily for groceries, or machinery parts, or shuttling the boys from various school and sports events, an endless string of errands. And Pauline had tried to convey her wisdom and experience. "This can be a man's world, Aimee. Look at the important jobs in our town, the judge, the doctors we know, the mayor and the builders. But us women have more freedom of thought. Our minds go thousands of miles further than men's do. We have no choice, what else would we do with our minds? You're a tough lass; I know that one thing."

Aimee realized that her mother had set this expectation, that seemed to have come from nowhere, that Aimee would depart that farm. Aimee would go out into the world and find more. Not only would her mind travel thousands of miles away, like Pauline's did hourly, but her body would leave the continent. Pauline wanted Aimee gone, not gone from her, but gone from this life, the only life Pauline herself had managed. Aimee understood that she knew much more about her mother than she'd ever realized.

She remembered this—her mother's hope for her.

16.

Jonathan's sister Emily came from Long Island to spend a week with him and Theo while Jonathan and Carly tried to hire a new nanny. Emily's company was effortless for Jonathan, like having an extension of himself. She slept on the pullout sofa, folding it up and tidying the living room before he even woke up. In the morning, while he got ready for work, she made Theo cheesy scrambled eggs, or oatmeal, or Eggos, and she prepared the French press, having it ready when Jonathan emerged from his room, ready to head out to work. Theo had to be on the sidewalk at 7:30 each morning to meet the school bus, and someone had to be waiting there at 4:00 p.m. to meet Theo when the bus pulled up. Jonathan was so grateful to his sister, he felt he could cry.

Emily happily made New York City excursions by herself, mostly Manhattan museums, in the hours Theo was in school, and she enjoyed sending off and receiving her nephew at day's end even more. They'd spend the two hours before Jonathan got home, playing and talking. Emily prepped dinner early so as to have those afternoon hours to fully devote to Theo.

On the first day, Theo bear-climbed the two flights of stairs to their apartment door. The cherry-red walker was waiting for him inside the front door, and for the first time in Emily's eight years of visiting them, they walked down the hallway to Theo's room together. Theo leading and Emily following with a one-step, pause, one-step procession.

Theo walked directly to his bed, turned around with the walker and fell backwards on the mattress.

He looked up at his aunt. "You like that?'

Emily stood facing Theo, she was incredulous. The pride in Theo's eyes and the smirk on his face were light years ahead of where he'd been at Christmas.

"Indeed. Very cool, Theo!"

"Want to play?" Theo asked casually.

"I would love to play with you."

Theo rolled over onto all fours, and then let his feet down backwards from the bed to reach the floor, inadvertently demonstrating for Emily how he had been taught to get back to his feet. His hands went from the mattress to grasp the walker. He righted himself and walked to his closet, looking at the shelves of games and toys for what he wanted to do with Emily first.

Jonathan had explained to her how tiring walking still was for Theo, that fifteen minutes of practice was the equivalent of him running for ten miles.

Theo had to be stopped at fifteen minutes. Even with his newly developing quads and calves trembling with fatigue, he had to be told to stop.

—

On her second night in Brooklyn, Emily watched from the sofa while Jonathan mixed gin gimlets for them from the open kitchen area.

"How many limes do you use per drink!" She called, not a question, but rather an observation.

"A ridiculous number. But they taste incredible." Moments later, he carried out the two tumblers, cloudy with lime juice and pulp with one large ice cube in the center. They sipped them in silence, except for their appreciative lip-smacks.

"That's tart."

Jonathan was so deep in thought about Aimee, about replacing Aimee, that he didn't even hear his sister.

Emily asked, "Making progress with finding someone?"

"I have four interviews tomorrow. If we're lucky, Carly can meet anyone great the next day, and we'll have a new sitter by Monday." He put his hand on his big sister's shoulder and squeezed it. "Thank you, Em."

Her presence there, on a moment's call, was typical of her generosity and of their relationship. He simultaneously expected the support from her and felt immense gratitude for it.

"It's easy. Sophia and Emmett don't really notice me after school anyway. It's honestly a bit of a vacation for me."

He squeezed her shoulder again. "Still. Thank you for giving us your week, for watching Theo. He loves spending time with you." Jonathan stared at the window. His thoughts traveling elsewhere.

"What else is going on with you?" Emily asked.

Jonathan was happy to be so well-known by her. "Actually, I'm looking at a career change."

"You are? How does a skyscraper engineer go about a career change?"

"I applied for a job with the Department of Emergency Management, disaster response in the metropolitan area. An engineering job, obviously. But a complete change of work."

Emily's face looked like he'd said he might relocate to Mars.

Jonathan laughed and swirled the ice cube in his cocktail before taking a sip. "After Hurricane Sandy and the flooding of Battery Park there's one billion dollars in federal funding for preventative measures. They're building flood walls and blue-belts, fortifying watersheds to help the city drain storm water. These projects can be beautiful too, revitalizing our wetlands. We might bring back some of New York City's wildlife of prior decades. Who doesn't like harbor seals and egrets?"

"You sound like you know this field already."

"I have an interview. There'd be plenty of on-the-job learning to do." Jonathan admitted.

"But the skyscraper. You're inseparable from it. You've been designing skyscrapers since you were five."

"No, I haven't. I took it up in college or even graduate school."

Emily laughed kindly. "Maybe you learned how to actually build skyscrapers then. But I'm three years older than you. I can attest that you were building skyscrapers with blocks at five. And if I tried to make them with you, you were a tyrant, yelling, 'It's not correct! It's never going to stay up like that!' And my block towers all toppled, and yours used all the damn elements you read about and every block we had in the house and those wood block skyscrapers would stay up for weeks in corners of the living room.

"Really?"

"Yeah!" Emily laughed.

Jonathan actually did remember what Emily spoke of. And also saw for the first time how tolerant his mother and sister had always been of him. His methods for doing things were sometimes immoderate, and his good-natured mom, and nurturing sister had never even teased him. They'd accepted him. His memories were bittersweet, realizing he'd had exactly what he hadn't given Theo. The family had seen him, understood him, and appreciated him. Because they loved him. He'd always given Theo the last, love was always there, but the others. The acceptance, exactly as he was? Theo had been jilted there. He was a flawed father. Not a father with a flawed son.

Thank god for Carly. Theo knew unconditional acceptance through his mother. And Aimee, Aimee had created the blend of the two of them, she was clear-eyed and demanding, and ready for Theo as he was. Aimee carried no baggage that Theo wasn't what she'd hoped for, and she wasn't here to accept the status quo either. Theo was going to have to meet his potential. Thank god, Jonathan thought, that these women figured out how to work around him.

—

Jonathan and Carly hired a new sitter. Rhonda had been a preschool teacher for nearly a decade. She exuded competence. She was young and broad-faced and looked like she could lift a car. She'd cared for twelve kids at a time and numerous children with disabilities.

Jonathan and Carly spoke over the phone, finalizing together that they would hire her, what the terms would be, what their scheduling needs were. There was nothing wrong with Rhonda; she seemed to be an ideal nanny. It had been easy, in the end, to replace Aimee.

"You sound glum, Jonathan." Carly said over the phone.

"I'm relieved. We have to hire a sitter. She's stable. She's just right."

Jonathan heard Carly sigh. "We need someone."

"It's fine. I gotta go."

Emily was taking the train back to Long Island on Saturday to return to her own family. Every afternoon that week she and Theo had played Trouble, pushing the plastic bubble at the center of the board to "roll" the die, moving the colorful pegs around the board, sometimes hitting *warps* that moved you across the board, or knocking each other out and sending the pegs back to home. Each action was a fine-motor skill for Theo, pushing the hard plastic bubble, tweezer pinching the peg and replacing it in a new hole. Theo played with enthusiasm and fast-moving fingers, but his aunt sensed a slight boredom anyway. She felt a bit like the babysitter she was, Theo waiting for his father's return home. Yet, Emily knew she had more time and attention for games than Jonathan did. He came home and warmly greeted Theo, but was quickly absorbed in making dinner, moving the household along.

They played the monotonous game this fifth afternoon without talking, Emily silently appraising Theo, wondering about his overall happiness. Not his motor skills, not his cognitive abilities, not his psycho-emotional health either. Wondering what *was* happy for Theo. Did it feel the same as happy felt to her? Did anyone's happiness feel the same?

"Are you having fun, Theo?"

"Yeah."

Theo kept the game going, taking his next turn, pressing the button down with his full upper body, counting the spaces out loud. "One, two, three, four. Where's Mee-Mee?"

"Aimee?"

"Yeah. When she come back?"

Jonathan had told Emily that morning that they'd found someone new. She now felt a flash of irritation toward her brother. Did Jonathan think Theo was a toddler whom he didn't need to discuss matters with? Did Theo know anything about the situation?

Emily pressed the bubble, wincing at its forceful popping. "I don't know."

"Aunt Em-ly. Is Mee-Mee in jail?"

"No, honey! She's not in jail. Why do you ask that?" Emily's hand covered her heart at the very thought of Theo's question.

"Police picked me up. Picked up Mee-Mee. Put Mee-Mee in jail. Mommy brought me home. Mee-Mee never came back."

"Aimee is okay. She's not in jail. But, Theo, you're going to have a new babysitter."

Theo looked at his aunt's ashen face and saw that she was now very sad. Theo knew that there were people who made his life change, people who made changes, and people who kept time. Em-ly would not be helping him bring Mee-Mee back. No one was helping him. Mee-Mee herself moved the air, made things shift. She made the energy in the house move like a ceiling fan stirred the air. She made the sounds and colors of the city sharpen and brighten and pop into sharp focus. She made time fly. She brought stairs, and music and how to use knives and scissors, and stand with ski poles and more than anything her song voice and seeing-eyes; she made Theo go. *Theo go!* It roared through Theo's head.

Theo stood from his wheelchair at the table. He took two fast steps towards the door and crashed onto the floor. His body lay in a combat crawl. He screamed, "Get Mee-Mee back. Mee-Mee! Meeee-Meeeee!"

—

Winter turned to spring in relative peace. In Jonathan's experience March usually came in like a lion *and* went out like a lion, still too cold. April was the cruelest month because it never felt quite like spring in New York. But this year was conspiring to make Jonathan physically comfortable. March did indeed go out like a lamb. Forsythia was everywhere. The crocuses broke away the last crust of snow and the daffodils appeared overnight. Jonathan walked around the neighborhood touching the velvety buds on trees. These dormant giants had appeared dead for months, and then, almost imperceptibly, their branches' tips fattened with nubs that would be leaves or flowers. Gray sticks became gray-green fingertips that one had to hover next to and actually touch, or be touched by, to fully perceive the transformation. A week later, trees were leafy again. Dogwood, magnolia and cherry trees burst with life. A re-birth so forceful and furious, that it held its own death in its glory. Blooms, by definition, were short-lived. The month of April bore all this transformation in the world, but the Brooks household was having its own dark season.

On Rhonda's first day, Jonathan left work early to meet the school bus with her and introduce her to Theo. He had planned to work from home through the afternoon, while Rhonda and Theo played and spent time together—his way of training and observing a new sitter. He'd be there for Theo, if needed, while he got to know a total stranger.

He'd introduced him to Aimee this way too. Theo had repeatedly crawled back to him for moments of connection before Aimee lured him away again.

But this time, Theo was behaving differently. He stayed in his room with Rhonda. He acquiesced to the board games Rhonda suggested. Jonathan stole down the hallway twice to peek and listen, to see how his child was connecting with this new nanny, who he didn't know yet himself.

Theo sat on his bed, his upright pillow with arms supporting him, while Rhonda perched on the other end of the mattress and they played Go Fish across the bed.

Theo's speech had become nearer to age appropriate in the last couple of months. He spoke like a four- to five-year-old, which was to say fluently, but with poor grammar and limited vocabulary. And he'd played this set of cards repeatedly; he knew the matching animal sets by heart. Jonathan felt no surprise to hear his son say, "Do you have a fox? Do you have a Narwhal?" Although six months ago, he would not have imagined these utterances. Rhonda glanced at him through the doorway but didn't draw attention to his presence. "No, I don't. Go fish." Rhonda was smiling and gave the impression she was enjoying herself. Jonathan crept away.

That night, Theo woke at 3 a.m. and screamed from his bed. Jonathan woke with a start. He was out of bed immediately and turned on the hall light outside Theo's room, to allow muted light into his room, and hurried in.

Theo blinked at Jonathan and cried a little as the dream let go of him.

"Did you have a bad dream, buddy?" Jonathan stroked Theo's hair.

Theo nodded. He struggled to sit up. "Aimee falling from skyscraper. Is it real?" Theo began sobbing and clutched his father's forearms waiting for the answer, "Was it real?"

"No, sweetheart. It was a very bad dream. Aimee didn't fall. Aimee is fine." Jonathan had no idea if Aimee was fine. A lump of grief sored his throat as well. "Everything's okay, buddy. You had a bad dream, that's all."

The remaining weeks of spring's furious onset went along this way. Placid afternoons with Rhonda. Theo cooperating in a way that quickly grew sinister to Jonathan. Was he placating him and Carly. Was he behaving for his captors. He imagined Theo was biding his time, as though he knew he had more patience than anyone else and would eventually win. But win what? Well he knew what. Because for the first time in his life, Theo had nightmares almost nightly. He awoke screaming in the middle of the night. He dreamed that Aimee fell into a hole, that Aimee was lost in space, that Aimee was dead, that Aimee was mad at him, that Aimee was in jail, that Aimee's legs broke. He dreamed that Aimee couldn't walk.

It didn't take a psychiatrist to understand that Theo had grown symbiotic with Aimee. He loved her and missed her. And the two of them had brewed a new mixture, a child and caregiver batter that formed a single dough, Theo and Aimee. What Theo could and couldn't do, what he wanted, or was it what he could envision, was inextricable from the Aimee who lived in his mind.

Jonathan became aware that at some point in the last two weeks the walker had fallen out of use. Theo used EZ to get around. He did not stand on his feet and clamber down the hallway.

He asked Rhonda about the walker. Rhonda flushed apologetically. "Does Theo use it? I thought only the wheelchair."

"It's okay, Rhonda. You didn't do anything wrong. I'll talk to Theo and Carly, and his physical therapist."

That night, Jonathan unfolded the sides of the cherry-red walker; he *tralinged* the Hello Kitty bicycle bell that was attached to it, and called out to Theo. "Buddy, let's practice walking. I haven't seen you use this lately."

Theo was at the dining table, seated in EZ, a dozen feet away from him. He toggled the joystick to the right with his right thumb, and the chair rotated to face Jonathan. Theo looked perturbed. He used the butt of his hand to press the joystick forward to come to Jonathan and the walker. His expression was one of minimum tolerance. Theo stopped before his walker, and like his father had, he reached out and rang the bell attached to its top bar. First just once, and then repeatedly. Over and over, Theo pressed the tiny brass lever, making the bell jangle it's tinny sound again and again.

"Stop Theo." Jonathan was suddenly annoyed.

Clumsily, with his feet, Theo lifted the footrests upright to each side, so he could put each foot on the floor. He hadn't bothered to position himself in front of the walker as was necessary. Perhaps he'd forgotten. Theo put his bare feet on the floor and used the walker, sideways, to pull himself up and out of the chair. The walker wasn't sturdy enough to bear his weight, and had Jonathan not been right there to grasp hold of him, Theo would have fallen backwards onto the rug.

"Whoa, boy! Not so fast," Jonathan tried to joke, as though Theo's behavior was eagerness. But he sensed it was something else. It was recklessness. The night before Theo had dreamed that Aimee left him outside and wouldn't turn to look while he called and called out to her.

While he held Theo around the waist in his left arm, he jerked the walker into the right place, directly in front of him. "Grab it, Theo. You know how to hold onto it and lean on it. Get yourself oriented."

Theo obeyed, but Jonathan could see immediately that Theo's hands were lax, his arms not bracing and engaging his muscles, as was required. Jonathan thought he detected that Theo's muscles had even shrunk. "Theo, you don't have it. Flex your arms. Use your muscles."

"I am." Theo forcefully pushed the walker away in a poor imitation of how to propel it before a deliberate step. The walker bounced on its rubber feet and fell forward without him. Theo leaned back on his father. "Get it for me."

Jonathan twitched with frustration. Theo was four and a half feet tall and fifty-seven pounds. He couldn't stand freely, unsupported. "Theo, I can't pick it up off the floor while holding you!"

Theo sank into his father, forcing Jonathan to bear his full weight. He called it quits.

Jonathan felt his temper rising. He saw the two of them from the outside, like a pair of broken dancers in a frozen ballet. His anger drained away.

"It's okay, Buddy. Let's try it tomorrow." He held Theo in his embrace.

17.

AIMEE WAS awoken by the buzz of a text. She turned away from the phone and toward the window. It wasn't morning anymore. Sunlight pushed itself against her thin curtain. It was another one of those full-on spring days. Why did the world insist on shining? Aimee didn't move a muscle, only her ribs rose and fell with her breath and she made no effort to do that, in fact she issued only the shallowest breaths.

Aimee had no money in her account. She hadn't been to school in three weeks. The abortion was four weeks ago. She had left Theo alone at the café six weeks ago. She'd last seen her family in Ireland twelve weeks ago. She'd fucked Connor ninety-one days ago. She had last been touched by her mother eight hundred and eight-four weeks ago.

She toed the bedsheets. A tiny gesture. Her foot sliding four inches forward, four inches back. She had found that this worked on other days to eventually get her out of the bed. She kicked with her eyes shut, her breath so short it was making her dizzy. Abruptly, Aimee stretched long, leaning backwards in bed stretching her abdominal muscles. When she was fully extended, she jacked her body further, until there was sharp pain. Since the abortion, there was a stretching point of her abdominals, of her very uterus, that caused a feeling of ripping apart. She did it several times a day, to feel that knife in her gut.

The text was probably Carly. She had called or texted Aimee every morning this week. Aimee waited to look, relishing the feeling of care that came with imagining Carly writing her again. Maybe she'd never stop calling as long as Aimee never responded. Not for the first time, she wished that Carly was her mother. This had begun at the police station, watching Carly rub Theo's back. Aimee admitted to herself that prior to all this trouble, the crisis, she had fantasized that she was Theo's mother, if anything. But that had morphed into wishing she was Carly's daughter. Cared for and child-like.

Carly's texts had said, *Call me please and let me know if you're okay. We miss you. I'd really like to talk to you. I'm thinking about you.* These messages, especially the voice messages, were the most comfort Aimee had these past weeks. The only comfort. She got out of bed each day between eleven and noon. She ate something, ramen noodles or a can of soup. She showered in the evening, around midnight, hoping to feel tired. She woke up tired and was awake at bedtime. Aimee knew she couldn't shake off this malaise, just as one can't shake off the flu, but can only ride it out.

She was depressed and yet she had no regrets about the abortion. She'd saved her own life. And now she was waiting to return to herself and take up that life.

Aimee sat up in bed and reached for her phone. Carly.

Hi Aimee, I could come see you today. Are you around?

It was nice to receive such a caring text. It might propel her out of her room faster, but she did not open her mind to Carly's actual offer to visit her. She imagined taking a shower and leaving the apartment, boosted with the momentum of Carly's concern.

Aimee held the phone forgotten in her hand and stared at the closed bedroom door. The phone vibrated, startling her with an incoming call.

'Carly Brooks'

Aimee felt caught, as if Carly could see her there in pajama pants and a tank top. Sitting on the edge of her bed, blood in her pajamas, a wreck. She needed help.

"Hi."

"Aimee? It's me, Carly, I've been trying to reach you for weeks."

"I know."

"Aimee. We all miss you very much."

Aimee nodded. A peep escaped her. The sound of the yellow baby chicks that scratched the dirt around their barn each spring. Aimee remembered how she used to sit cross-legged in the dirt, making a hammock of her cotton skirt. How she'd fill her lap with baby chicks. A bowl of fluffy, hopping warmth.

"I have the day off today. How about I come by for a visit? Are you home now?"

"Yes. I'm home." Aimee started to stretch herself toward the ceiling, arching, but stopped before the ripping sensation. "Please come."

Before Carly arrived, Aimee showered, found a sanitary napkin, got fully dressed and put her dirty clothes and sheets in her laundry bag. Her apartment was a studio on Lincoln Place. Carly would see all four walls. Aimee made the bed with the second set of sheets she owned. She piled dirty dishes and pots in the sink and wiped down the counter. She tidied up the room. Lastly, she opened the window. She waited for her visitor.

When Aimee opened the door for her, she saw that Carly carried two tote bags, one with a bouquet of daffodils poking from it. Aimee's gaze rested on the luminescent flowers.

"It's tulips and daffodils everywhere. Isn't this yellow other-worldly? Almost neon."

"Like baby chicks."

Carly tilted her head appreciatively. She put both her bags down, and hugged Aimee.

Aimee had waited four weeks for that hug, or six weeks, or twelve weeks, or eight hundred and eighty-four weeks. She didn't know anymore.

"Aimee, what did you decide?"

"I had an abortion."

Carly nodded. She inhaled and exhaled and kept nodding. "Are you okay?"

"I'm relieved its done." Aimee didn't know what she might say next. *I have no money, I'm not going to class, I've lost my job, I am not myself.* She shrugged, her mouth set and her chin trembling. Carly hugged her again, holding her until Aimee separated herself, several minutes later. Aimee wiped her eyes and took a deep breath.

From her tote bag, Carly brought out a bean and vegetable soup she'd made, a crusty baguette, a box of blueberries, two large chocolate-chip cookies. She laid this picnic on the small table by the window. Aimee washed a pot out of the sink and Carly warmed the soup on the narrow stove.

After they had eaten in near silence, Carly put up hot water for tea and washed their lunch dishes and all the other dishes in the sink, while Aimee talked from the table. Carly didn't dare respond or even look at Aimee who seemed to be in a trance, speaking to someone else, no mystery who. Her accent was so thick and her vocabulary full of Irish slang that there were whole sentences Carly couldn't make out. Carly stole a glance at Aimee as she spoke, noting also that she looked thin, paler than usual, that her eyelids were red, with dark circles beneath them.

I never properly mourned my mum. You died—she died on me, quite literally it seemed. Not just abandonment, but I felt de weight o' yooehr body on me lap, on me torso whenever I was still. I tried to never be still, which is easy on a farm, you know. De unrelenting needs o' animals from sunup to sundown can keep away a ghost. Father didn't speak o' you to me. Me brothers never uttered your name. I never saw me brothers cry. De never saw me cry. We didn't 'ave a proper cry fer you. We didn't 'ave final words, no goodbye, no last bits o' advice for yer only daughter.

But it was dere anyway. It whispered in de horse's tails when I groomed dem out. It spoke in rushes when de brook thawed and began moving again in Spring. Yooehr voice came down in torrents and pounded the metal roof over de hay shed with every hard rain. Yooehr voice spoke to me when I rode me bike to Connor's. When I made out with 'im in his jeep, at de movies with 'im, on top of de covers on his bed. When I moved to Dublin and I cut off twelve inches of me hair. Me hair dat you always untangled an' braided. I heard yooehr voice along with de breath of dat hair landing on de floor.

Yooehr voice spoke clearly to me when I drove de jeep home drunkenly from his wedding. Dat horrible deed done. His seed already working in me body. You said the same thing every single time, for all those years, Mum. You said, *Leave. Go, Aimee. Find yourself out dere. Find your meaning, lass. You're free to go, me child. You're free."*

Aimee bent over her knees and wept for herself and for the baby she didn't want and for Pauline, whose voice she'd never stopped hearing even as she believed she'd forgotten it entirely.

Carly kneeled in front of Aimee and held her until the torrent stopped.

—

A week later, Aimee returned from a class to find a small package in the building vestibule. The cardboard box with a postal label from Castlemaine immediately caught her eye. She lifted the feather-light package with two hands. Her father's cursive handwriting on the cover, *Ms. Aimee O'Malley.*

Aimee ran up the stairs to her apartment with the package. She grabbed a kitchen knife and gently slid it under the tape to unseal the box.

There was a folded piece of lined white paper on top and without even lifting it, Aimee could see the blue satin of her mother's dress beneath. She put the paper aside on her kitchen table and gently lifted the dress. She closed her eyes a brief second before looking at the dress front, remembering her own soiled hands, covered in chicken grease, wiping this delicate fabric along her stomach as if it were a worthless napkin. She remembered stepping on the dress in her bedroom before falling asleep, and leaving it in a corner of the room in the morning when Colin drove her back to the airport, her head pounding from so many glasses of Champagne the night before, from the bitter aftertaste of regret.

Aimee opened her eyes and examined her mother's nicest dress. The blue was unstained and unwrinkled. She imagined her father gently scrubbing it with his laundry brush, using baking soda and seltzer. She knew he'd pressed it too. The dress was restored and renewed. She hadn't known she still wanted her mum's dress. But her heart lifted as she held it against her in her small, bright Brooklyn kitchen.

Dear Aimee,

You forgot to pack the dress. It looked so fine on you. Mum would love to see you now as a young woman yourself. A year from June you have a graduation in New York City, if your old man can still read a calendar correctly. Would you be too embarrassed if your brother and I came to watch you take up that diploma? There's never been an O'Malley doctor and it's no surprise to me that you'd be the one, Aimee.

With love, always, your Dad

Aimee's mouth hung open. And from that dumbstruck expression, she heard her own laughter break the silence. These two would not embarrass her at all. Her family would see *her*.

—

On a Sunday evening, Jonathan entered Carly's apartment without bothering to knock. She was expecting him. He was picking up Theo after he'd spent the weekend with Carly.

"I'm here." He called out.

Carly approached with a smile, she held a stretched canvas against her stomach, the backside facing him. "I have a present for you."

"For me?"

"I don't know why I didn't think to give it you sooner." Carly wheeled the painting around, shyly displaying it to him.

It was the portrait of Theo at age two in the bathtub. Hair slicked back, light brown from being drenched with water. Carly had captured the wetness on his skin. Jonathan remembered seeing this painting the night Carly had shown him all of them. It was the only one he was "in." His shirt sleeves were rolled up, and his arms framed and protected this seal of a boy, smiling up from his tub. Only Jonathan's arms were in the picture. He could remember the moment. It was his favorite of the group of paintings.

"I love it. And I'm delighted to have it."

"Really?"

"Of course. I'll hang it today." Jonathan took the canvas from Carly's hands and held it before him. He stared at it, lost in thought. What's right for Theo is the same thing that's right for everyone. The people around him behaving naturally. For Jonathan, that word captured something elusive that he'd been searching for. Cutting Aimee out of Theo's life had been based on her making a mistake. She'd left Theo unattended. But it was unnatural to then make Theo utterly abandoned by Aimee. And to make Aimee pay forever for a mistake. They had inflicted this greater pain on Theo. He wasn't even hurt by Aimee's abandonment. It was their excising Aimee from his life that had made Theo truly suffer.

Carly had left Jonathan three years earlier to survive. Jonathan had always thought it was to survive their fate as parents. Theo's intensive care occupied Carly's days fully. As did the sense of loss of Theo before the encephalitis. When did Carly ever take a breath, a tiny pause from mothering Theo, until the day she moved out?

But Jonathan had been wrong. Carly didn't flee Theo or the never-ending fight to help him become himself. Carly had to leave the man who saw the world from a place she couldn't even visit. Being with *him* and being Theo's mother were an unnatural mix. Everything Carly tried to do became a fight. Because he was living a different story than she was. Carly never stopped her herculean battle with Theo's obstacles. She just realized that she could do it better alone, without carrying Jonathan too. It now seemed perfectly natural. She'd extricated herself from another burden, in order to do the work she was committed to. It all made sense to Jonathan. He thought he knew what could be right for his family now. He was willing to try.

"I have a proposal."

"You're proposing?" Carly cocked her head "Should I put on a fancy dress?" She was confident enough in the knowledge that Jonathan was not asking her to re-marry him that she could make this joke.

"Of a sort." He opened his arms in a gesture that only Carly would recognize as requesting a dance.

She stepped into his arms and put her hand on the small of his back, the other hand grasped Jonathan's outheld hand. They began to dance without music. No music and no fancy clothes. There was no ring in his pocket. Both of their wedding rings were tucked away in drawers.

"Carly, what if we move in together. We get a brownstone where we can each have our own apartments. Theo can live with both of us again. We can help each other. We can be together, but apart."

"Live in same building? Carly continued to sway, with a measured space between her and Jonathan, distant enough that she could see his face and carry on this conversation, but still holding hands, bodies touching.

"Yeah, further east in Brooklyn, see what we can afford. It's just a thought. But I've thought it through a bit."

Carly laughed then. "Oh, I know that. You've never skipped the thinking it through part. I bet you've even looked."

"I've resisted."

"Good for you. We can think it through together for a change."

Jonathan took a step closer and rested his head on top of Carly's. "Let's think about it. I don't know if it's a great idea. Maybe it is." They swayed more than they danced. They faced opposite directions, both with their eyes shut.

Carly leaned backwards to look Jonathan in the face again. "What if the place has three separate apartments?"

Jonathan puzzled a moment over her words. Did she mean what he thought? Was she thinking of what their family had grown into. What was natural. Jonathan nodded. "There could be room for one more."

He kissed his ex-wife goodbye, and with care, carried her painting out.

—

It was a committee who interviewed Jonathan. It always was with government. They each had a sheet of paper in front of them. Which Jonathan knew was an approved set of questions, and that he would be scored on his answers. Jonathan had begun his career as a skyscraper engineer working for the Department of Buildings sixteen years earlier. He could have earned three times as much money by working for one of several major contracting companies that build skyscrapers, the blue whales of buildings, in New York City. But he'd always liked the responsibility of government, its role in the construction of a metropolis. They stood to make no profit. It was their entire role that these buildings were done right. Were mathematically correct. Were solid and economical. Jonathan paid extra attention that they were elegant too, and fitting to the neighborhoods where they would reside. It might surprise some people that the state of New York employed architects and engineers. But state employees, who tended to be lifers, knew that these many departments; Health, Homeland Security, Energy, Buildings, employed all kinds of professionals, doctors, scientists, meteorologists, architects and engineers.

It was Jonathan's best asset for this new position as an engineer in the Department of Emergency Management that he'd been working for the state for sixteen years. And it didn't need to be said by Jonathan or the five other men and women in the room who interviewed him that his pension would transfer over to any state department. These infamous pensions were why state workers were lifers.

They'd been kind enough to lay the sheet of questions before Jonathan as well. "In case you're a visual person." The British man leading the interview had joked, they all were. Jonathan knew this man would be his direct supervisor if Jonathan obtained the job. On first impressions, he thought this man would be a very good supervisor for him.

Jonathan had already spoken at length about the Jetson, and about three other skyscraper construction projects he'd managed in the last eight years. He'd spoken of his commitment to green construction and the environment and his history of collaboration with the Department of Energy. The Department of Energy, a frequent partner of his past, now held the shadow of Sara Danner for him. Not quite anger anymore, but distinct displeasure.

"You've had an illustrious career at great heights. You're used to working fifty stories in the sky, on the geometric design of a structure that will consume two acres of the city, the precision and to be blunt, prestige. This work is significantly more down to earth, in the mud puddles of the city if you will."

Here Jonathan reached into his briefcase and pulled out seven drawings he'd done in the last six weeks. It was high summer, and Jonathan had taken advantage of the longer days and of having Aimee back in their lives, to kayak the waterways around the city. His Forester now had roof racks, and in the corner of the living room, where once a blue foam staircase had loomed, there was propped a sit-on-top yellow sea kayak, dubbed "the banana boat," by Theo.

"It's a big part of the appeal to work more down to earth and water. These are sketches of breakwaters and blue-belts that I drew up from seven key locations around the city: Red Hook, Battery Park, Brooklyn Bridge Park, at the foot of the George Washington Bridge, North Williamsburg, the Verrazano, and the narrows of Manhattan between the Manhattan and Brooklyn Bridge including the South Sea Port. The weather will continue to be more unpredictable ... will continue to be what was previously unnatural. The wind and waves will interact with New York City in more invasive and aggressive ways. I'm a pre-emptive designer. What we can do as engineers is prevent future destruction, limit damage by anticipating the ways nature might behave. Hurricanes are part of the city's future. Rising tides, storms and mega waves will be occurring if not every year, at least every few years. I've researched the projects forecasted by this department and I am very drawn to the work, the management and the prevention of emergencies or curtailing of them. When ocean and river water strikes the low-lying parts of Manhattan, the waterfronts of all five boroughs, it's not so different actually than engineering for strong winds that we know will pummel skyscrapers. These designs for breakwaters will diffuse the water and separate it into lighter and smaller streams that drift backwards to their source, broken up upon impact with the modified land, land modified with drainage vents, very similar to how we confuse the wind that pushes against skyscrapers."

Allan Chambers pointed to a sketch made along the southern tip of Staten Island, he tapped an underwater view of a three-dimensional shelf beneath the partially submerged breakwater, that Jonathan had included in his hand drawing. "Is this an oyster bed?"

Jonathan felt the hint of a blush warm his face. "Yes."

Chambers pushed each sketch around on the table while Jonathan spoke. He'd studied each one, that featured a unique design to the shape of the shoreline. Jonathan had sketched a layered perspective, showing the construction projects that would lay beneath the water line, concrete breakers nestled into the sand of the city's two rivers, as well as a view of the surface which resembled sieves, or colanders or woven mats, and other designs still that reached into the sky with sheaths of metal that protected highways that were less than fifteen feet from New York's Harbor, like the BQE as it made its way to the Verrazano and a great stretch of the West Side Highway. Many of these lofted structures also contained windmills, that Jonathan had dreamed might produce enough energy to power the lights that would shine upon the river to illuminate evacuation routes, perhaps much more energy. The drawings also depicted voluminous plants, native grasses and shrubs, who's roots would hold the banks together, ease the shoreline more gradually into the rivers, increase backflow of water, beautify the city, clean pollutants from the waterways and increase the city's wildlife of birds, ducks, fish, eels, waters snakes, possibly even oysters, otters and seals of earlier eras in these waters.

"You're a skillful artist." Chambers respectfully pushed each drawing into a long row where he could look from one to another, and then push them individually to his partners around the table. I'm also intrigued by your perspective. The point of view appears to be from a seated position, in the water." Allan Chambers moved his electric wheelchair several inches toward his nearest colleague to push the drawings toward her.

Chills ran through Jonathan's skin. He had not noticed that his potential boss, the department head, was seated in a wheelchair until that moment. He took it as a sign. Jonathan wanted this position badly.

"I drew the initial sketches from a kayak in the water."

The interview wrapped with a question about the required travel. "Is three to four trips a year manageable for you?"

"Yes, I can manage it. It will require advance planning though. I have a son with special needs. However, I live with my ex-wife and our nanny, so we have things pretty well covered."

And with that comment, made to a group of his future colleagues at the Department of Emergency Management, Jonathan shared more about himself than he had in the prior seven years at work.

Theo

OUR HOUSE has three stories. Each floor tells its own story. My room is on the garden level so I don't have to do too many stairs. But I did stairs before most everything else. Mom's room and her studio are on the ground floor too. The backyard is outside our kitchen, and I can go out alone. Dad is one floor above us. He says it's the best floor, and he deserves it because it was his idea to buy the house. Mom shakes her head and smiles when he says this. His eyes are happy most the time. But he makes tight eyes when I play my music loud, or get sassy, or when Aimee tracks mud in from her vegetable garden and doesn't even notice.

Aimee lives on the top. She watches me in the afternoons until mom or dad come home.

When she first came back to me I thought she really had been in jail. Her eyes were all different. She didn't see me all the way, like she had before. Didn't see all the things I was still waiting to try. There were purple boats under her eyes and her eyes were underwater with the boat bottoms.

I tell Aimee what I see.

"Mee-Mee, you're not going to get anywhere with eyes under-water. Mee-Mee, you're my only babysitter now. It's you again."

When Aimee finally listened to me, she said, "I'll never leave you again Theo. Not like that. If we ever part, I'll say goodbye. I'll always tell you if I'm leaving."

"Can you stay until I grow up?"

"Maybe."

Aimee never lies.

Aimee watches me the way she used to again. Not full of feelings about who I will be. Just looking to find out who I am and what I need to learn next.

I can see what Aimee needs too. I tell her, "Go see your friends tonight." Or I tell Aimee, "Go to your garden." Or if it's snowing, I say, "Put on some music for us."

Aimee says, "You're alright, Theo."

"You're alright, too." I say.

We laugh.

When I graduated from fifth grade, I crossed the stage with my walker to get my diploma. Mom, Dad, Emily and Brad, Sophia and Emmett and Aimee, all cheering in the front row.

A week later, we watched Aimee cross a stage and get her diploma. She wore a long black gown and purple hat and a green and white sash for Ireland. She waved her diploma in the air at me. She hugged her dad and brother and then hugged me for a long time after.

"We made it." I whispered to her.

Acknowledgements

The members of my time-tested writing group read and commented on many evolving drafts of this book and helped me to find the story's final shape and truth. Anne Hellman White, Leland Cheuk, Emmeline Chang, Kim Liao, Jennifer Sears, Jael Humphrey, Roja Heydarpour, Jill Dearman and Laura Catherine Brown each continue to give me companionship and trustworthy direction on what can be written better. They mean so much to me on this writing journey.

I read many books during the writing process that fed my imagination and ignited my desire to tell a parent's story of raising a child in unmarked territory. Most notably the memoir, Blue Sky July, by Nia Wyn and Brenda Saughnessy's, Our Andromeda both inspired me deeply.

I am eternally thankful to the band of people at Vine Leaves Press who keep the home fires of this independent press burning around the globe: Peter Snell, my first reader, Melissa Slayton, my editor, who brought fresh eyes to the project and inspired great improvements, and especially the founder and Publisher Jessica Bell and Publishing Director, Amie McCracken, who bring artistry and professionalism to the publishing of their books, and are just so cool.

Thank you to Cathy Shields, my sensitivity reader, for adding her personal knowledge and experience, and perspective on the book.

My aunt and uncle, Penny and Tsvi Akiva, have always been there for me, beside me and at my back, since the day I was sent to their doorstep at fourteen, and they made me part of their brood. It shouldn't surprise me, yet it does, that they came to my aide full-force, to read this book in its final revisions, in seeming hours, with focus, love, and fierce conviction that the story had a place and a purpose. I'm so grateful for their support.

My kids, Enrico and Gael, make this publication all the sweeter for their enthusiasm and excitement. Kids are better than their parents, and these two keep me trying my best to live a good life.

Loving thanks to my husband, Bill. My final writing step is getting his take, and mostly taking his advice. I thank him for another deep dive into the artistic abyss with me. No matter what, he's there to celebrate every accomplishment of mine and to throw a party.

Vine Leaves Press

Enjoyed this book?
Go to *vineleavespress.com* to find more.
Subscribe to our newsletter: